# DON'T ANSWER
## WHEN THEY CALL YOUR NAME

Ukamaka Olisakwe

Griots Lounge Publishing
Canada

Published in 2024 by Griots Lounge Publishing Canada
Copyright © 2024 by Ukamaka Olisakwe
Genre: YA Fiction
Cover Art by Sarah Peters
Interior Design by Rachelle Painchaud-Nash
ISBN: 9781738699322

Printed and bound in Canada

# DON'T ANSWER
## When They Call Your Name

Ukamaka Olisakwe

# Prologue

## MBIDO

**OUR** story begins on a farm.

It was the year of the white yam, and Big Father was pleased with his harvest. Mother was not.

Big Father was a man of great height and resolve. A dedicated farmer, he had broken the hard soil and ridged the land. He planted his yams and when they had germinated, their tendrils creeping towards sunlight and tangling with each other, he drove stakes into the soil and watched as the plants curled around them, reaching for the sky. It was the healthiest yam farm in the whole of the universe, one that stretched from one end of the world to the other.

The yams flourished. The roots gobbled up the manure fed to them and they spread their hands, the tendrils thick and fat—the width of a baby's hand. Weeds sprang from the earth and tried to suffocate the yam plants, and Big Father pulled every one of the weeds out and dumped them in a pile to whither. After he was done, after he irrigated the land and fed it cow dung and dead things—organic fertilisers that nourished his precious crops—and after the yams grew without impediments, birthing tubers as fat as toddlers, he stood back and breathed, pleased with the work of his hand.

Big Father had a wife—Mother—who was eager to help, and who wanted to join in the farming of the yams, for she came from a race of industrious and ambitious women whose stories travelled the universe. But Big Father rejected her help. He gave her a small piece of land far from his yam farm and said she must only cultivate female crops, like cassava and cocoyam, what mothers before her had done, and which to him were suitable for a woman.

Mother was furious. The first child of her parents, she had worked her father's yam farm and made profits from selling the rich crop. Her father did not mind that she preferred to work on the land; he did not mind that she kept the profits she made after trading her harvest at the Universe Market; he did not mind that she did what sons were meant to do because she was his only daughter, and he would bend some rules to make her happy. He had initially insisted she work with her mother on the female farm, but Mother was a stubborn, cocky sort of child who did what she wanted. Her great-great-grandmother was Ifejioku, the mighty deity responsible for yams in their world, and to whom farmers prayed before and after they harvested the noble crop. But over time, men took over the responsibility of farming the crop, appropriated it, declared it "the male crop," because it had become a household staple and because they had gotten fat off the wealth they made from it. They dedicated their sons to the service of the crop and called themselves *Njoku*, rising to the position of nobility in their communities.

Mother fought against this, insisted she must farm the crop. Her father tolerated this until she saw her first blood, then he quickly plucked her from her farm, audited all she had amassed for herself, and divided them among her brothers.

"But, Papa," she protested.

He shut her up with a raise of his hand and reminded her that a girl would always leave her father's house and move into her husband's, where she would start her own family and raise children, where she could do as she pleased and manage her own affairs. Mother did not care about marriage or children, but the idea of doing as she pleased in her own home appealed to her, and so she obediently agreed to marry Big Father.

She danced energetically on her wine-carrying day. She smiled into the faces of her brothers, who had bought for themselves the rarest jewels and the finest silks from the proceeds of her hard work.

"Watch me flourish," she told them as she left their world and moved in with Big Father on his vast farmland.

The sight of the blooming yams welcomed her—their rich green leaves, the properly manured ridges, the irrigation paths Big Father had crafted. She stood on that land, on the first day of her new life, and something lifted in her chest.

"This will do," she muttered, then tilted her face to the sky, where she sensed that her brothers were watching. "Watch me flourish," she said again.

Her marriage began to disintegrate in less than a year.

Mother stood on Big Father's farm and hissed at the rich crop taunting her with their fat, healthy green tendrils. She was nineteen years old and she didn't want a child yet. She wanted to become a successful yam farmer and trader, just like the mothers before her who were famous for their exploits at the Universe Market. Getting Big Father to give her some seedlings or even allow her to venture into yam farming had become a major problem. And yet, despite her desperation, Mother would not beg; she was beautiful and arrogant and stubborn, and she tended to sulk. Her father would scramble to indulge her, to get her to smile for him, not her husband. Big Father did not bother to ask why she sulked, why she hissed when he walked past, why she would not share his bed, why months passed and she refused to farm female crops.

A neighbour noticed the rivalry between husband and wife and offered to hear their grievances, to make peace between them. But Big Father did not care at all; he would come home from the Universe Market and sit in the middle of their compound and spread out bags of jewels, his returns from the sale of his yams. That haughty display of wealth was hard to miss, making Mother angrier. When it became clear that he would never approach her to make peace, that her emotional fits would not break down the walls he built around his heart, she stopped sulking.

Mother was stubborn and arrogant all right, but she also had a good head on her shoulders. She knew that to get what she wanted, she would have to find a way to break down Big Father's walls, to make small compromises so that she would be happy in his house, so that she would regain all she had lost to her brothers on account of marriage. She waited until the harvest season was over and harmattan had come and gone, and the rain had poured and prepared the earth for farming again, before she went to Big Father with a great plan.

There were many stories about Big Father depending on who you asked. Some said his mother, The First Mother, suffered many stillbirths and so the creator, Onye Okike, built new bodies until they found the one who gave them children; that The First Mother finally gave birth to Big Father after a lifetime of trying; that the creator gave Big Father a farmland, which was this world, on the runt of the universe, to cultivate chosen crops and populate the earth. They said Big Father worked it so assiduously, broke the hard soil and made much profit, more than all the other children, that he acquired more worlds from his siblings that stretched from one end of the galaxy to the other; that the humongous size of his estate was why everyone began to call him Big Father. He was a ruthless man, they said, who guarded his acquisitions jealously and was merciless towards anyone who trespassed on his property. His mother was buried in this world, not on the hallowed grounds where Onye Okike and the first mothers rested and so he loved this world like a child would their living mother. The stories about him were numerous, but they all agreed on one thing: Big Father would never budge on matters concerning his yam farm. And this was why he did not care for his wife's petulance.

But Mother was undaunted by the stories. She had set a goal for herself, and with that, she went to Big Father's quarters, at the front of their vast compound, bordered from hers by a short ogirisi fence. The distance between their quarters was a day's journey. The dust whorled that morning as she set out, sweeping red upa into the air, tinting everything brown-red. Coconut trees flanked the entrance of his quarters, and birds pecked away at the overripe bananas dangling from the squat trees on either side of the compound.

She knocked on Big Father's door and waited. She should not have had to, but she had been angry with him for a long time, and it had been months since she shared his bed. So she felt like a stranger again, just like she had felt that day, one year before, when he came to their house to ask her father for her hand in marriage. It took a moment, and then she heard the shuffle of his feet, the heavy thud of his steps as he approached the door, and then he stuck his head out first, his brows meeting at the middle in a quick frown before a teasing smile spread over his fine face.

"This one you have decided to show up at my door, I hope everything is fine o," he said, clearly resisting the urge to laugh.

She clenched her teeth and clasped her hands behind her back. She wanted to punch his face. "I am well, my husband," she told him. "I have an important matter I must discuss with you."

He laughed again, leaned against his door frame and folded his arms. "Ehen? What is this important thing that finally dragged you out of your hut to my quarters at this time of day?" He looked at the setting sun, the orange glow washing into his yard. He raised a brow in mischief, stared at her hard. "Have you finally decided to return to my bed?"

"Yes," she blurted, out of breath.

"To give me children?"

"On the condition that you will let me farm yam crops."

He straightened up, dark clouds rising in his eyes. "You can only farm female crops."

"Listen, you are no longer a young man," she said. "You have to start thinking of the children who will take care of this place when you can no longer do everything by yourself."

Her submission caused him to laugh, a loud cackle that shook the very ground she stood on. "Look," he said, "when I am desperate for sons who will take over from me, I won't have to beg you. I can easily find women who will be willing to do what I want."

"Good luck finding anyone as resilient as me. Do you know the mothers I come from?"

"Your great-great-grandmother is Ifejioku. We already know that."

"Yes! And we do not bend for anyone. We never succumb, no matter what. This is what you should want in your children. Children who would stubbornly defend your territories from those vultures you call brothers, who are waiting for you to keel over so they can take over your properties."

Big Father reddened in the face. "No one would dare!"

"You have no idea how jealous people are of your wealth."

He breathed hard, his nostrils flaring. "You will not put ideas into my head, do you hear me?"

And she stood her ground, lifted herself to the tip of her toes so that she matched his height, so that she met the fire in his eyes with her rage. "Your mother did not give up—"

"Don't you dare talk about my mother."

"I never ever give up. Isn't that what you would want in your children, a race that never ever succumbs, no matter the challenge life throws at them?"

Her words got to him. The mention of his mother always got to him. He turned abruptly and returned to his hut, his words carrying out from the dim room before he slammed his door shut.

"Go home. I have to think."

She waited for his response. She waited for days, then weeks. And just when she thought she might have to pay him another visit, he showed up on her front yard one early morning, breathing as though he had raced the entire distance to catch her just as she stepped outside to wash her face.

"Four sons," he said. "You will give me four sons. Then you can have whatever you want and do whatever you feel."

"Four sons," she said, nodding her assent. "I will come to you when my body is ready for your children."

And with that, she returned to her room. She held her joy tightly inside, tried not to sing out loud, until she was sure he had left, until she was alone again. And then she lifted her voice in a melodious song that carried out into the universe. Her music trilled for days.

Mother knew the best time to conceive sons; mothers who came before her had taught their daughters. They counted days after their periods, they knew the best time to get a boy, when to hold a girl. They could tell the sex of the baby from the feel of their breasts, the severity of their morning sickness. Mother felt all these, and when the time came, her first son, Eke, slipped into the world with a lusty cry.

"Here," she told Big Father, who wrapped the baby in a soft ogodo. "You have your first son. Three more to go."

"You have done well," said Big Father. "You will have everything you ask for when you have given me four sons. I am a man of my word." He smiled. "I always keep my promises."

Mother got pregnant again within two months. She wanted to hurry through the process. Her body broke and swelled; her skin felt like a strange cloth she was trapped in, and she no longer knew how to wear it. Her yard was filled with the cries of her always-hungry son, Oye, and her nights were short. But then guests started pouring in from the worlds, bearing gifts of rubies and gold and diamonds and oils and scents. She welcomed them with smiles. She showed them her baby. She swayed in dance when they sang ceremonial songs for her. She drank the hot soups her mother prepared and took her sitz bath religiously. She told everyone that she was fine, but when she retreated into her room and closed her door, she slumped on her bed in fatigued grief.

Still, she brought her husband two more sons—Afo and Nkwo. The last boy came at dawn, when the moon was closing its eyes in sleep and the sky hung like thick grey hills. Big Father lifted his boy, smiled up at the bawling face, and said, "You have done well, my wife. He is beautiful and perfect."

She sat up and cleaned herself. She put away her birthing clothes and washed and oiled her body with udeaki. She lined her eyes with otanjele. She scented her body with oils. After she had adorned herself as she remembered she used to be, even though a lot had changed in her appearance—her breasts were fuller, her hips wider, and her periods were heavier—she still had her mind set on her goals. She went to Big Father and asked for yam seedlings and an extra portion of land. Harmattan had come and gone, and the rains had fallen and prepared the soil for farming.

Big Father leaned against his door frame and squinted at her. "Our sons are still too young. Who is going to take care of them when you go to the farm?"

She took calming breaths. She would not let her rage overtake her cool demeanour. "We will employ good nannies," she said.

"Nannies? To raise my children? To teach them whose values? No way."

"We had an agreement," she reminded him.

"And I have not changed my mind. All I ask is for you to stay at home a little while, until our babies are strong on their feet, then you can have your yams and farm any portion of land you choose."

He retreated into his hut and before he would slam the door shut in her face again, she noticed something different in his mien—the smirk on his face, a proud set in his shoulders, and the steel in his eyes.

On the week of their son Nkwo's tenth birthday, Mother came to a realization about Big Father: He would never let her farm yams. He would never allow her to have what she truly wanted. He would keep making demands, stretching the years, until she had grown old, until motherhood had wrung her out.

Big Father threw the boy the best party in the universe, drawing people from far and wide to jolly with him. He employed the best caterers. He slaughtered the fattest cows. The grown-ups partied on the eve of Nkwo's birthday until the following afternoon. They sang and drank and ate and danced. When they had exhausted themselves, their children took over in the afternoon, music booming out from the compound into the universe. Everyone noticed. Everyone stopped by to pay their homage, for Nkwo was Big Father's favourite and would later have the biggest market day dedicated to his name.

Mother watched all this from the corner of her eyes, offering bright smiles whenever people hailed her. She danced when they sang for her. She laughed when they called her a "strong, great woman." She carried her rage inside, bound it tightly against her body with her fine ogodo—the rarest akwete wrapper, a gift from her mother on her wedding day. She did not talk to her husband or go to him when he waved her over to come and dance with him during the jewel-spraying time. She watched him with their son, her body swelling with bile as they danced in circles, as the guests sprayed them with the finest and rarest jewels mined from exploded stars.

The following day, after the guests had packed up and returned to their worlds, and she had cleaned her yard and fed her children, she went to Big Father's quarters, tightened her hands into fists, and brought them down on his door. She banged with all her might and only stood back when she heard his angry voice from inside.

"Who the hell is pounding on my door like that? Have you gone mad?"

And when he threw open the door and saw her, he sighed and hissed. In his hand he gripped a famous machete, lights shooting over its glinting surface, the same electricity that had climbed into his eyes.

"Have you lost your mind?"

"You never planned to keep your end of our bargain, did you?" she said.

He put the machete away, and his eyes returned to normal, dull and human. "You must wait until my sons have grown into men."

"Your sons," she said, and smiled a sad smile.

Her words perhaps stung him, because he inched closer, and when he spoke again, his tone was grave. "You must wait until they are old enough to take wives, then you can go ahead and have whatever you want. That's what a good mother is supposed to do."

Her eyebrows shot up, veins popping on each side of her temples. She had expected him to deny the accusation, or even find a way to soften the blow, to consider her feelings despite everything. But his bluntness cut deep. He might as well have spat in her face. She wondered if he was really that heartless, that selfish, the vilest person to whom she had given the best years of her youth. She should say something angry in response. She should throw a fit, hit him, or worse, grab the machete and take a swing at him.

But she only smiled and nodded. "I have heard you, my husband."

Even though her mind was going in circles, roiling with thoughts, webbed with rage, seeking the best and perfect way to get back at him, this man who stole her best years and tricked her into bringing him children when her mind was not ready to take on the responsibility of motherhood, when she wasn't even sure that she wanted to be a mother.

"I will wait until our sons have become men, then I will farm the yams," she told him sweetly and went back to her hut.

It took two nights of thinking, two nights of her staring at the ceiling, listening to the sounds of night outside her window, playing scenarios over and over in an endless loop in her mind, reaching deep inside her to imagine what the mothers before would do in such a situation, what they would do to a man who snatched their youth, and condemned them to an unhappy marriage. And then she arrived at a solution that she was sure would ring for the ages in the entire universe.

The following day, she waited until the sun had risen to the base of the trees in the east, when she was sure that Big Father would have left for the Universe Market, before she took her sons to her own hut and locked them inside. Then she marched to Big Father's farm, stood in the middle of the vast land, and looked at the sky. That afternoon, the clouds were a brilliant white, and the sun shone with a burning passion. She closed her eyes and summoned in her mind the map of the universe, whose paths she had learned when she was only a child. She listened, her mind tracing the orbits of other worlds, the position of the stars, the direction of the moon, the glory of the sun, and finally, the floating asteroids tumbling endlessly in the vast space. She tracked their dimensions with her mind, seeking the perfect one whose targeted fall should obliterate the farm without dragging its devastation to her doorstep.

It took a moment, before she sensed it, the debris from a dead star, buzzing past. She stilled her mind and reached deep inside where her rage sat boiling. Taking a deep breath, she stretched out her arms, arched them to the point where the asteroid floated, and let out a sharp cry, a sonic burst that pierced through the sky, bounced into space, and pulled the asteroid towards their world.

Her pores burst open. Her nose flared. Her chest heaved. The clouds groaned, darkened, blocking out the sun. The wind whorled, and birds flittered from the trees, flapping and flapping, winging out of the path of the catastrophe. She did not open her eyes as she pulled, as she dragged destruction to her husband's precious farm, where he buried his mother—the grounds he worshipped and elevated and loved more than life itself.

The asteroid hurtled towards earth, carrying fire in its tail.

She moved away from its path just in time. And when it hit, the force lifted her into the air and rammed her back to the earth, knocking the strength out of her. Then the force rippled in waves, in a wide circle, obliterating everything in its wake. The thunder of its destruction reverberated throughout the universe.

Mother lay on the ground, drained. Dust covered everything. Her ears were ringing. The earth was still shuddering. She heard her sons' cries. She heard the discordant voices of people arriving with rescue vehicles. She sat up slowly, looked around her, and saw that she was in a cavernous valley the asteroid had excavated. And the yams were gone, their leaves and tendrils now charred corpses smoking in black death.

She was thinking: Where were her sons? Were they okay? Then she saw Big Father descending into the valley, his footsteps heavy, sad, angry, emotions that slowed his gait and hunched his shoulders. He gripped his machete tightly in one hand.

"What have you done?"

His voice rang with defeat, the tone of one whose world was done, all hopes dashed; she had reached into his throat and ripped out that which he cared for most above all things.

She looked at him and felt a smidgen of pity for him, this stubborn man who had sealed his ears against her plight, mocked her with his success, and pushed her to the wall, until she was forced to throw all fists at him, anything at all, to hurt him just as he had done her. The lights in his eyes shone so bright that they glistened with the tears that rolled down his cheeks. They rippled across his skin and turned his complexion into lightning, his voice clapping like thunder.

"What have you done to my mother's grave?" he asked again.

She should be worried. She should be filled with remorse. She should get off her bottom and talk to him. She should do all those things women were expected to do to quell their husband's anger. But then she remembered the mockery, the taunting, his satisfaction in her misery.

"Now you don't have yams and I don't have yams. No one has yams. So, we are even, aren't we?"

She began to laugh. She had wanted to cry. She wanted to wail about how her life had turned out, how her marriage had finally disintegrated into tatters, to wail that she regretted what she had done but would do it again if she could. But when she tried to cry, all that spilled out of her was laughter—searing, mocking laughter.

"We are even now, aren't we?"

She laughed and laughed. She was still laughing when she saw it—the swing of his machete. It happened in a flash. He did not allow her a second to catch her breath. She only gulped as the blade rushed towards her head. Then a quick slash. Pain exploded in her eyes. A scream split from her throat. The world turned black. And she was falling into a deep, dank void.

# One

# AJA

**THE** winds were swift when we set out for the stream that morning. Obi walked beside me, clutching the handle of his tiny bucket in his mouth. No other kid was on that bushy path that led to the stream, not even an adult. Night had stretched without ceasing and dawn was taking too long to come, even though our cock had already rung the alarm twice. It was in the middle of a vicious harmattan, and the winds rattled window shutters, the walls so cold, red dust fogging up the air. I tightened my quilt around me. I had layered myself with good sweaters—my father's old sweaters—but still felt a bit of the chills seeping through the pores, sucking at my knuckles. A bird chirped from the trees and Obi turned in that direction, dropped his bucket, and barked at it. I laughed.

"It is just a bird," I said.

He picked up his bucket again, moving even closer to me, his body pressed against my right calf. Obi was of medium height, but he carried himself like a giant and had a voice that could make you pause. His skinny body was the colour of fresh clay paired with white, his tail curled with fur. He trusted me, was always protective of me, and would plant himself in front of me whenever he sensed that something was amiss. I rubbed his head and muttered that every-thing was fine.

"We have to fill the drum before everyone wakes up," I told him. "We don't want what happened yesterday to repeat itself, do we?" The stream was crowded when we got there the day before, and a fight had broken out among the girls after Chinelo shoved Okwu-dili. They grabbed each other, throwing hands, and the other children gathered around them, hooting and clapping, blocking out the path. I pushed someone out of my way. They swung at my head, and Obi lunged at the girls, dispersing the crowd. Our priestess, Nwanyi Ndala, came and chased everyone home and locked the entrance to the stream with omu stalks. No one dared break the omu until evening when she announced that we could go ahead and fetch water again.

"No more fighting," I told Obi. "That's why we must fill the drum on time, okay?"

He made a sound, an agreement. My brother. I could never think of him as merely a dog because Obi understood things and carried himself better than the dumb character given by which our people described dogs. Adults thought dogs should sleep outside, eat outside, remain ostracised from the family because they saw them as guards, not sentient beings, who loved and cared, who had feelings, who understood when you were distressed and needed company or distance. Sometimes I imagined that Obi was my little brother come back to life, who died a mere few days after his first birthday. My mother rarely talked about him and I wondered if she never did so because there was no point talking about what barely stayed.

Our people rarely talked about what they lost anyway. The men and their sons worked on the yam farms and the women and their daughters cultivated female crops and vegetables. The soil was often hard, and farmers prayed for the rains, then prayed that the dry sea-son would not stretch too long and kill everything in the ground.

The heat was intense and the leaves were yellowed. Mama said this place used to be a rainforest and had rich soil and a kinder sun. But our world had gradually changed, and things got worse. The soil bleached of nutrients because of constant dry season fires, and the sparse rain that hardened the soil so that it took much effort to break. We bought fertilizers from wealthy traders in rich villages who corralled themselves away from us and our misery. Not that we cared about mingling with people who turned up their noses at us when we walked past.

We entered the narrow path that led to the stream. The water would be clear this morning, I was sure, and in an hour, it would become muddied by feet rushing in to fetch from it. The entrance was demarcated by a short wall, one side leading to the women's side of the water, the other side meant only for the men. Our people had rigid rules for the stream: A girl must never fetch water from it when menstruating; a new mother must never fetch from it until three months after the birth of her baby; no one must come to the stream when sick; no one must come when afflicted with skin diseases. So many rules, some good, but some did not make sense. Like, why should a girl stay away when menstruating? I had yet to see my period. My breasts had only just begun to bud, and my nipples were inverted. Mama said that it never used to be this way, this late puberty, that our bodies perhaps were mimicking the conditions of our land. This used to bother me. My peers who budded breasts early and saw their first blood took to mocking girls like me, saying hurtful things. Once, Ekwutosi picked a fight with me at the stream after I called her out for cutting the line.

"I don't talk to small girls like you," she had said with a scoff.

Her friends had burst into raucous laughter. They pushed their chests out after they hefted their buckets, so that their nipples poked against the thin fabrics of their clothes. I'd learned to ignore them and spent more time at the village square, where I played football with my friend Eche and his peers. They did not mind that I was the only girl who played ball with them, and they tackled me like I was an equal, which I really liked.

But the water was gone by the time I reached the stream. It was just dry, cracked land, like clay after it had sat in the sun too long. The trees bordering what used to be the stream looked parched, their once-green leaves terribly yellowed. Even the birds that often sang from the trees were gone. Heat was rising from the soil, choking the morning air.

"This is not right," I told Obi, backing away.

I knew what had happened, but the strangeness of it all muddied my senses, the fact that this was truly happening in my lifetime—this phenomenon that had cost our village so much, the reason our parents walked hunched, as though they carried burdens too heavy for their fragile bodies to withstand.

"Come, Obi," I said, hastening away.

We had just gotten to the demarcation when I saw my friend Eche coming out of the men's side of the stream too, his eyes wide with horror.

"The water is gone," he said, his voice so small.

"Yes," I said, my heart pounding. "What does this mean?"

"You know what it means," he said.

He stopped, bent to rest his hands on his knees, gasping. Eche was tall too, tall for a thirteen-year-old, fair, wide-shouldered, and wore all those features as a child in oversized clothes. He was ruthless at football but tender in other things. He cried easily, sulked easily, and now he was out of breath. I had to touch his shoulder and urge him to breathe.

"They are going to do that to us," he said. "Offer us as an Aja to the bush to make the water return again, won't they?"

"Stop talking nonsense," I said and pulled him up. "Let's hurry home."

We walked in silence. We did not tell each other the sequence of events that the disappearance of our water had set in motion because we already knew and talking about it was needless torture. It was the tenth year since the last child was sacrificed to the bad bush as an Aja to atone for our sin. Everyone knew the story: how the great Mother had sinned against Big Father and as punishment he banished her into the bad bush. And in that fit of anger, he declared that her children would forever atone for her sin, or they would be wiped off the face of the earth. And so, every ten years, an Aja was sent into the bad bush and to make sure that we never forgot when it was time to perform the sacrifice, Big Father dried up our stream, creating a Plague of Famine, until an Aja was sacrificed. And the Aja had walk to the furthest end of the Forest of Iniquity to Orimili—the heart of the water, which was the source of our stream—and walk back. If they succeeded, they were allowed to return to the land of the people, our Ani Mmadu. If they reached Orimili but failed to make it back home, then nothing would happen to us; we would only have lost yet another child. But every Aja must reach Orimili, or the journey was useless. And the punishment for failing to reach Orimili was a stretched-out famine and an extra Aja who had to come from the deserter's immediate or extended family. Only three people had successfully returned from the journey. The last person, a girl, was our priestess's great-grandmother. I was only three years old when the last Aja, a boy named Chuba, was sent off. When he didn't return, his father died from a broken heart, and his mother married a man from one of the rich villages and moved away. No one talked about that sordid story. No one spoke about our punishment. Perhaps we stopped talking about it because we hoped Big Father had forgiven and forgotten about it.

Now we walked in silence, my heart already weighed down by the sombreness that hung heavy in the air. When we reached our settlement, Eche muttered a goodbye and headed down the bumpy path that led to his house. Obi and I turned right.

Mama was taking out last night's ash from the tripod in the outkitchen when we entered our yard. Our house was a squat two-bedroom bungalow with peeling paint and a rusted roof. The walls had cracked from the harmattan, and there was a layer of red dust clinging onto everything. The front yard was littered with the leaves from our kerosene mango tree, and the bananas beside the house, next to Mama's windows, were dying.

We made for the back of the yard, where I could hear Mama singing an ancient tune as she did her chores, the dust of the ash rising into the air, the *shh-shh-shh* of her short broom grating the mud floor of the kitchen, drowning out our footsteps. Mama was bent over, long breasts barely contained by the ogodo she'd knotted under one arm. She looked so young, yet so beaten by stress. She once told me she married Papa right after she turned sixteen, and I came along barely a year later, a fat hairless thing that sucked her breasts like I had starved in all the months I spent inside her. That story made me laugh. Mama always found a way to make everyone around her laugh, but she had lived through the toughest times in our village, had lost her siblings to the punishment, and lost Papa barely a year ago.

"Mama," I said.

She heard me and stood up, a smile entering her tired face. "Adam," she said, with her soft lilt at the end of the syllable. But then the smile quickly died when she saw my empty bucket, when she took one look at Obi's pail and saw that it was empty too. "What happened?" she asked, hurrying towards us. She was out of breath, her chest already heaving, and I knew that she already knew the answer even before I opened my mouth.

"The stream has dried up."

Mama's hands flew to her throat, her jaw slacking, revealing the gap in her teeth. She stared at me for a moment, light draining from those big eyes, and I feared she had gone into a shock. I had never seen her like that before. But she broke from that state, dragged me into the house, and slammed the door shut, locking Obi out.

"But, Mama—" I began.

"Shut your mouth right now or I will shut it for you."

She looked like she was on the verge of losing her mind. Mama could be gentle and loving but she could be a terror too, especially when she was in panic mode. One time, when I was playing football with the boys and fell and twisted an ankle and passed out, I woke up to find her yelling at me, slapping my face, pulling me to her chest, expressing such a chaotic mix of feelings all at the same time. That was what she was doing now, dragging me into the room, yelling at me to shut up, protecting me from the terror she knew was coming, all at once.

"Not again," she said as she pulled the shutters, as she peeped out of our window, as she listened to the air, seeking out the danger that was sure to come for one of us that morning.

Obi was barking outside and I wanted to tell her to let him in, but I knew her well; Mama could hear nothing at that moment but danger, a danger she must protect her child from, no matter what it took.

"Not again," she kept muttering as she dragged everything shut, as she looked around the room for any sign of threat. "Not again."

From the crack in our window, I heard mothers and fathers yelling their children's names and dragging them inside. The news most certainly had spread. Death had come again, and no one wanted their beloved to fall into its claws. The rules for the Aja sacrifice were messy. In the past, the Aja designation was rotated according to age, until it became too contentious. Then it was rotated among the families, until those who had only one child fought it to the ground. Nwanyi Ndala introduced various methods, and none seemed to work. They created mortal enemies with friends taking the battle to one another's front door because of the easily faulted system until Nwanyi Ndala consulted the divine and returned with an answer: Big Father would summon an Aja through her staff. This new system seemed to work perfectly because no one had dared push back against it in over fifty years. Whatever parents did to protect their children from the punishment was almost always a waste of time.

"Don't come out until I say so. Don't answer if anyone calls your name. Even if you are dying or want to pee or move your bowels, you must do it inside this room. Are you hearing me?" Mama shook like she had caught a fever. She pulled the blinds closed. "Do not set foot outside until I return, do you hear me?" she said.

"Okay, Mama," I said.

And she frowned. She did not believe me. She looked around her room, searching for a sign that said I was lying. She peered at the corners, at the ceiling, behind the curtains. She looked under the bed, under our table. When she didn't find the lie, she hurried to the window and pulled the shutters. She walked out of the room and found Obi in the passageway, barking. She grabbed him and he made a small whiny cry. She brought him into the room and dropped him on my lap, and he sat on his haunches and barked at her, his way of saying he was not happy about how she snatched him off the floor like an old rag.

"Good boy!" I wanted to tell Obi, but I knew Mama well. I knew what she would do with those big hands of hers if I so much as opened my mouth and said what she didn't want to hear just then. She was jumpy and nervous, her body visibly trembling.

She wagged her finger at me again. "I don't want to see your ghost or even this dog outside. Are you hearing me?"

She did not wait for my answer. She banged the door shut as she hurried off, and I heard as she turned the key in the lock, walked down the passageway, and locked the main doors. I knew she put the key in the tight space inside the left cup of her brassiere, her favourite hiding place, where she used to hide all her money, including the cash our neighbours gave me on my last birthday. She had promised to buy me new shoes with the money. I never saw the shoes, not even the laces.

Nwanyi Ndala arrived shortly, stamping her divine oji on the ground, the *jigirin-jigirin* sound of the metal staff piercing the sudden still air. She was the only surviving child of the last Aja who returned from the bush. She never married and never had a child of her own, perhaps by choice. I couldn't imagine what it would be like to nominate your own child as a sacrifice because of an ancient sin that the god still held the world accountable for.

The priestess's arrival was announcement enough. Parents soon trooped out of their houses and marched to the gazebo, where she stood waiting to begin the great ceremony. Through the crack in our window, I could see straight into the meeting place—the small grove where our parents often assembled once every month to discuss communal issues. I could not hear what Nwanyi Ndala was saying to the grown-ups gathered around her, but I imagined that she must have sung something in the line of: "It is the time for the great atonement, a time to ask the god to forgive the sin of our mother, so that he will return our water and our farm will flourish again and our souls will not perish in this cursed world."

Our parents stood, shoulders hunched, listening to her long speech. They always humbled themselves before the priestess whenever she had cause to visit them. Perhaps they stood that way because they feared her. Or maybe it had something to do with her oji, tall and strung with pieces of red cloth and beads and metals and other mysterious items that made unearthly sounds when she stamped it on the ground. Eche once said that Big Father sent the oji directly to the priestess from heaven because the oji saw the truth. It fished out those who did terrible things. Like last year when someone stole Obiefuna's goat, and Nwanyi Ndala brought the oji to the gazebo. When she ordered everyone to hold the oji and tell the truth about what happened to the goat, Obiefuna's youngest brother, Ikenna, fell to the ground, carried his hands up and began to cry. He confessed that he sold the goat and used the money to buy anklets for his girl-friend in the rich people's village.

I was terrified of that oji. The first time Nwanyi Ndala brought it into our house was some months after Papa died, when his brothers tried to steal his land from Mama. She refused to let them have it. She chased Uncle Ifedi off that land with a machete when he went there to harvest the yams Papa had planted. She knotted her ogodo tightly around her waist, grabbed Uncle Chijoke by the legs, and slammed him on the ground when he too came to steal our crops. Everyone began calling that land 'Oguno' because of all those end-less fights, until Mama went and brought Nwanyi Ndala to judge the matter. Papa's brothers ran and never tried to claim our land again.

Nwanyi Ndala held the oji the same way she did that day when she came to our house. She talked in that loud and slow way, as if she used her tongue to count her teeth, before she spat words out of her mouth. Our parents stood before her, nodding in unison, heads bobbing up and down like agama lizards. They did not hold her gaze. They stared at their feet. Even Papa Chinelo, who enjoyed shouting at his wife and Papa Oge, who always yelled at us when we kicked our football into his compound. All those adults, who often hissed or muttered under their breaths whenever they saw me playing football with the boys. They stood in the middle of the square, bowing before Nwanyi Ndala like she was a god, listening, humbled by her fierce presence. I pressed my ear against our window, straining to hear what she was saying. But the winds had quietened.

Outside, Nwanyi Ndala raised her oji high and brought it down, chanting a feverish prayer. The sky groaned. The winds howled. She stamped the oji again, the metals catching the sun and shooting fire in all directions. Some of the lights washed in from the crack in our window. I pushed it open a little further because I was fascinated by her magic and also because it was funny to see the frightened look on the faces of those annoying men. The lights danced on our walls, on the floor. And Obi, who had been bored all this while, started to bark and jump around, excited at the lights.

"Obi, tone it down!" I whispered, but the dog was so happy. Plus, Nwanyi Ndala was not done raising her oji and bringing it hard on the ground, the lights spreading in delicate waves that covered everything.

Everyone knew how an Aja was selected: Nwanyi Ndala summoned the child with her oji. She didn't need to go to any house to choose who would atone for our sin; her oji did the choosing. How it did it, we did not know. All we knew and all I had heard was that she would come as she had come today, perform the divination, and an Aja would walk out of their house and come to her.

Parents hid their children. Mama too. She locked the door, which was funny to me. Why would I want to offer myself as an Aja? Why would any child willingly offer themselves and for a crime they did not personally commit? I pulled the window shut a bit more, just enough to see into the gathering, and enough for the lights to keep Obi distracted.

By this time, my attention was divided between the priestess and Obi, whose barking had grown more frenzied. One moment I was staring at the performance, and the next, before I could even say, *hey!*, the lights began to retreat, and Obi hurled himself onto my lap and dove outside with them.

I didn't even wait to think about what I should do. There was no time to think. I just knew that Mama would flog me mercilessly if she saw that dog bounding towards them. I just knew that my butt would be on fire that afternoon. I knew that Mama, tall and massive like she could crush three men with her arms, would deal with me for breaking one more rule. So I leapt right outside with Obi.

Mama saw us and froze. "Chi'm!" she cried, her hands clutching her breasts, her mouth going slack.

I stopped running, my knees suddenly turning to rubber. I wished for something to happen, for a curtain to fall from the sky, and hide me from the glare.

"Aha!" said Nwanyi Ndala in my direction, with this wide smile. "Aha!" she said again. "Big Father has chosen the perfect one. Big Father never lies!"

The other parents visibly sighed in relief and lifted their heads again, the previous weights letting up their shoulders.

"Chi'm," Mama said again, tears leaking out of her eyes.

Obi had stopped running. He returned to stand with me. The air suddenly became too cold, and I shivered in it.

"Chi'm," Mama said again, making towards us, putting one foot slowly after the other, as though the ground was fragile and she would sink into the earth if she stamped her feet too hard. "Chi'm!"

Nwanyi Ndala's face was a shining mask of joy and relief.

I looked at the sky where birds flapped about, and I wished I could turn something backwards, so I would not have jumped out of the window.

The other adults disappeared into their homes. I couldn't tell how they all left, but when I looked around, it was just me and

Mama, who was now begging Nwanyi Ndala to spare us. I looked at Obi. Panting with his tongue hanging out, he sat on his haunches like a good boy, staring at Nwanyi Ndala.

"My daughter, stop crying," Nwanyi Ndala said to Mama. "Big Father does not make mistakes. What you should be doing is thanking our Father in heaven for this kindness. What if no child came out? Or have you forgotten the war that ripped families apart three Ajas ago, when my oji didn't summon a child and we had to cast a vote?"

"But she is my only child!" Mama said. She was on her knees, keening like an animal, rocking back and forth. "My only eye. She is all I have in this world."

I didn't know what to do with myself. I looked at Obi, who still sat like a good boy, and I wanted to pull his ear or wag my finger and tell him he was no longer my friend—anything to make him understand that he was the reason I jumped out of the window. But the truth was I couldn't blame Obi for this new trouble I had gotten us into because deep inside me I knew I should have stayed away from the window. Now the damage was done, and Nwanyi Ndala was talking to Mama in the way adults did when they consoled snivelling children.

Looking at Mama again, I went on my knees. I begged the priestess to leave us alone. "It was a mistake," I told her. "I only came to get Obi."

Mama's voice climbed over my own. "If you take her away from me, what do you want me to do, kill myself? It is better I die. Better that than to lose my only eye."

"Taa! Do not spit taboo from your mouth," said Nwanyi Ndala in a grave tone.

But sorrow had taken over Mama's mind. She cried harder than she did last year when Papa did not wake from his sleep. I tried to say I was sorry, but when I opened my mouth, only sobs poured out.

Mama crawled over and pulled me to her breasts. She wrapped me tightly. She rocked me back and forth. Obi began to bark and from the crook of Mama's arm, I saw that he was growling at Nwanyi Ndala, his teeth fully bared. If he looked ready to launch an attack, the woman didn't care. She raised the oji, light sparkled from it. And just like that, he shut up and started to bounce around, butting his nose on the ground, trying and failing to gobble up the lights. I wanted to pull him by the ear and call him a bad dog.

"We have to go," said Nwanyi Ndala, grabbing my arm. "Evening will soon be here. We don't want to waste a moment longer."

Mama held me, refusing to let go. She chanted, "Ewo! Ewo!" Her tears soaked into my hair.

"Uchenna, let the child go."

"No," Mama said.

I tried to snatch my hand from the woman's grip, but she dragged me out of Mama's grasp with a force that belied her frame. Mama finally let me go.

"Come," the priestess said. "We don't have time."

I told her to leave me alone. I pulled away from her, and she let go of my hand so readily that I wondered why she had been insistent only a moment ago.

She dropped to her knees and looked at me levelly. "Well, Adanne," she said, "you are the only one who can save us now."

"I want to stay with my mother," I told her.

"You could, but would you want her to die?"

I didn't wait to think about the implication of her words before I said, "No."

"Because that's exactly what will happen if you don't answer Big Father's call."

Mama whimpered, but I couldn't look at her. The damage was done. And much as I regretted disobeying her, I didn't want her to

die. I would rather she had another child and lived. She had suffered enough and had fought too many battles since Papa's death.
She deserved to live.

So I stood up and followed Nwanyi Ndala out of the gazebo.
Obi was right there by my side, and Mama followed behind, her gait
laboured, her feet dragging over the hard, dusty ground.

As we marched out of the square, the sun boiled the earth, and the
heat burned through the soles of my sandals. It was like stepping into
the hot coals in Mama's tripod. It had always been like this with us:
the heat, the merciless sun, the occasional rain, the vicious harmattan—everything in the extreme.

Most of the houses on our side of the town had no fences, and
their walls were bare, rarely painted. Some of the windows had no
louvres, and the compounds had no gardens, no fancy coconut trees
flanking their entrances. The yards were crowded with yellowing
banana and plantain and coconut and orange and guava, any plant
that produced seasonal fruits and vegetables and could survive the
heat, so that families would have enough to eat and preserve until the
sky opened its mouth again and farmers cultivated new crops.

I looked back and tried to catch the last glimpse of our home. I
could see the short fence and a narrow entrance crafted from dwarf
ogirisi trees, and the house Papa built two years before, after selling
one of his lands. He used some of the money to buy an old Peugeot
pickup. The truck sputtered and quenched six months later. Papa
took it to the mechanic workshop on Ife Street. He never got it back.

We entered Okwu Village where big houses sat like bullies, their gates bordered by tall palm trees, the compounds furnished with green hedges. They also had fat tanks filled with the water drawn from pipes they laid all the way to the stream, so their children would not have to trek the distance to fetch like we did. Mama once said that the pipes cost ten times whatever our entire village would be sold for. Same for their tiled front yards, the short brick fences, all displayed flagrantly as if the owners wanted us to see their opulence and wither with envy. People on this side wore foreign clothes and spoke a stilted Igbo—the Igbo of those who had acquired new languages they prided as superior to our old tongue.

A boy bounded out of one of the houses, laughing. A girl chased after him, aiming a green water gun at his back. Their clothes were bright and pressed, their skin consistently oiled and supple, as if they never stayed in the sun too long, as if they were constantly fed butter and eggs, not cassava. They saw us and paused their play. The boy leaned over and whispered something to the girl, who stared at me, and I wished I could see into her mind to know what she was thinking, why she looked at me as though I was nothing. I wondered if they woke up every day with a smile, knowing that they would never be offered as Aja to the Forest of Iniquity. Their great-grandparents invented solar cells that powered their homes and preserved their seasonal foods. They also invented fertilizers that nourished their crops and helped them grow quickly in a short time so that the people of Okwu Village were able to harvest aplenty before the scorching sun incinerated whatever remained in the ground. They battered tiny portions of their power and fertilizers with our village for Ajas and dumped the excess in their heavily guarded valley as waste to keep them rare so that we would be perpetually dependent on them for survival. And our people, knowing we had no option and knowing our land was useless anyway, signed the agreement.

This was why Nwanyi Ndala only ever came to our village when it was time to send an Aja off into the Forest of Iniquity.

It was perhaps why the rich kids watched with pity as we walked past, why they whispered into each other's ears. I straightened my dress, patted down my hair, wondering how I looked from their perspective. I stared at my feet; my toes and heels were caked with dust in my sandals.

"We are almost there," Nwanyi Ndala said.

I sighed with relief as she turned a corner, away from the curious gazes.

Mama walked with her eyes half-closed, her face swollen from crying. Her nose was running, and she blew hard into one end of her ogodo. She looked so dishevelled, so unlike her. A nail had been pulled out of our floor, and everything was crumbling. This would not have happened if I hadn't opened the window, if I had learned to obey rules like she had warned me all these years. A lump swelled in my throat, and new tears began to gather in my eyes. I wished again that I could turn back time so that I never would have gone near that window.

"We are here," Nwanyi Ndala said as we entered the small bushy path that led into her yard.

Her house sat on the flatland by the stream and the boundary between our village and the next. It looked from a distance like it had sprouted from the ground. But as we approached, I saw that it was just a big hut, so old it had tangled itself with the roots of nearby trees, the weed vines crowding her premises, everything meshed like those bird nests you would find in the trees at the back of our house.

The shrine sat beside the house like an outkitchen, a small mud grotto draped with dried raffia and palm fronds. Ornaments and wood carvings sat on the dusty floor, the walls decorated with chalk markings, the door so low that one would have to bend if they needed to enter inside and pay homage. Two wooden chairs were propped at either corner. They were low, like something built for a child, and I couldn't imagine Mama sitting on them. It would be like sitting on the floor itself, what with the tiny square seating and the short, sturdy legs that looked like those yam tubers Papa used to harvest from his farm.

Nwanyi Ndala sat on the bench by her front door and patted the space beside her. "Come and sit, my child. We have to wait for the eagle's arrival."

I stared at her and stared at Mama, who had settled on the foot of the guava by the entrance, her legs stretched out in front of her. She had stopped crying but looked so desolate and lost, her gaze focused on the sky above. And I wished again that I had heeded her warning. A different child would have been chosen for this journey, and their parents put through the torture. Not my mother.

"Sit," Nwanyi Ndala said again.

I sat. She shook her head, suppressing a smile, as Obi walked over quietly and planted himself by my feet, his ears flattened, and his tail tucked between his legs, as if he too was about to be sent on a journey.

The priestess did not waste time. "You must follow the flight of the eagle. It will take you to Orimili."

"Where will I find the eagle?"

"The eagle will find you," she said thoughtfully, reaching for something inside her shoulder bag.

"What if I get lost? What if something happens and I don't catch up with the eagle's flight?"

"Big Father works in mysterious ways. Getting lost might just be what you need to reach your destination faster. Do not doubt the feeling in your own gut."

I hissed and looked away. My gut had done nothing but put me in trouble, if only she knew the half of it.

"You will succeed," Nwanyi Ndala said suddenly. "I can feel this in my belly."

She must be mocking me at this point, I thought. Was this what she said to all those children she sent off to their deaths? Butter them up with hope, make them feel less afraid, before sending them to a fate unknown? My heart thumped faster as she spoke. There was a small, stubborn part of me that wanted to hold on to hope, to believe that I would complete the journey and return. She said I would make my people proud. She hung a piece of jewellery made of white marbles around my neck. She said I must throw it into Orimili on reaching my destination, that it was the only way to show that I had truly completed the journey, so that I would be granted passage home. She said these things very slowly, in the tone adults used when they lured children into doing something they were not ordinarily brave enough to do, like that time Mama found a cockroach crawling on our kitchen wall and started heaping me with praises, urging me to take a broom and squash it. But when the cockroach spread its wings and flew towards her, she had fled, screaming like it was the devil. I touched the marbles. They were fine stones, so smooth I would have been tempted to swallow one if I had found them when I was a small child.

"Do you have friends?"

I thought of Eche and his big, stupid laugh. Eche was terrible at football, but he always celebrated more than me whenever I scored a goal, as if he carried a joy for me that was too much for his body to contain. He sometimes joined me to go to the stream, even went to the bush with me to collect firewood. He was the only friend I could think of, the only one I knew would worry once everyone realized I was gone. I wondered what he was doing at that moment and if he had peeked out of a window too when the priestess came. I told myself he probably did, but I also knew that Eche always sat when you told him to sit and toed the line when you dotted a path for him. "Look at your friend," Mama once told me. "Why can't you be like him?"

"Do you have friends?" Nwanyi Ndala repeated.

"I have one."

"Good," she said, but didn't tell me why she had asked.

Maybe her way of reminding me of the important people in my life who would also be rooting for me. I didn't like this though; it felt manipulative. Bad enough that I was hounded by guilt for bringing Mama so much pain. Now I was to worry about Eche too? I refused to look at the priestess when she got up and spread a ceremonial mat on the ground, the kind our elders used when they offered prayers to our gods. I refused to look at her even when she sat and asked me to join her on the mat.

"I don't want to sit," I said.

"My daughter, sit."

There was a firmness in her tone, and a new steeliness in her eyes. She passed a glance in Mama's direction. I followed her gaze and saw that Mama was seated on the dusty ground, her knees now drawn up, her head bowed. I had never seen her in this state before, hopeless and dejected. I could not bear her disintegration any longer. I wanted to be done with it all, to get away from here so that the sight would no longer torment me. So I sat on Nwanyi Ndala's mat and told her to hurry up.

"Why is the eagle wasting time?" I blurted.

She ignored me and brought out her afa and splayed it on the floor. Obi crawled into my lap and rested his head on my thigh. I patted his head, and he shut his eyes, his breathing heavy as if he was about to fall asleep. But his ears perked up as the priestess began to pray, as she flipped the beads, chanting prayers and questions.

"Do you know that when I asked Big Father to bring out the one who would go on this journey, the sun didn't catch in my oji?"

she said. "The sun only reflected on the ornaments when I asked Big Father to bring us something the chosen one loves so much. And your dog came running." She patted Obi's head, and he nuzzled her hand. "You will take him with you."

"Okay," I said, relieved. Happy, even.

If there was someone I would walk through the dark with, it was Obi. He always sensed my mood, always knew when I needed him to snuggle up to me on stormy nights, always knew when to leave me alone. I pressed my face to his head as the priestess resumed flipping the beads, speaking to the air, calling on the winds to be swift for me, for the sun to be kinder, for day to stretch a little further, and night to shield me from its horrors. I held Obi tight to me and for the first time since everything happened, I began to believe that I would succeed on the journey. It was still a small, faint feeling, but it lifted something that had been pressing me down, and I was filled with new energy.

"She will go, and she will come back," Nwanyi Ndala prayed. "She will return in good health because Big Father himself has chosen this one in the most unusual way." The priestess's voice carried into the trees and rustled in the leaves. "Let's get you ready," she said. And without waiting for my response or agreement, she pulled me with her to the back of the house, still chanting her prayers, still wishing me well. "You will go, and you will come back. Our water will be replenished, and our land will be fruitful again."

We stopped beside a lean-to under which clay pots were stacked in a row. She brought out one of the pots and poured water into a basin. She returned to get a loofah and a bar of soap, then a tray holding udeaki and trinkets and combs. I wondered if she was really going to wash me like a baby when she lifted my dress and pulled it over my head in one swift tug.

"Hey, hey," I said, protesting.

But she said, "*Shhh*, there is no time. We have to hurry."

She pulled down my undergarments and tossed them into a corner. She scooped water from the basin and poured it over my head. The water was lukewarm. It took a moment before the chilly winds clashed with the water and a wave of goosebumps washed over my body. She poured more water, countering the chilliness, until I adapted to the temperature and the bumps retracted under my skin.

"There," she said, "you should be fine."

I nodded. She dipped the loofah in the water and rubbed the soap hard against it until it foamed and then she began to scrub my body, hard, peeling every layer of dust, every smudge of dirt off my skin. She was tender, but then my anxiety had returned, my eyes pricked with the beginning of tears. Why did I go to that window? Why didn't I just sit on the bed or distract myself with something unexciting? Why was I always drawn to trouble? None of this would be happening if I had learned to sit like a girl and act like a girl. My mother wouldn't be out there, her heart broken yet again, barely one year after losing her husband.

Nwanyi Ndala perhaps caught the shiver that ran through me because she paused the scrubbing, a sympathetic cloud dimming her eyes. "We must prepare you. It is the rule. You will like your dress," she said with a smile. "It is made from the finest akwete."

I tried to settle into the warmth in her tone, but I did not feel any better. I was comforted by the fact that she cared, that she did not treat me like those goats our parents slaughtered during festivals, such as during our Ede Aro. When Papa was still here, he would bind the goat's legs and pull its neck up before slashing it with a sharpened knife. The goat would thrash about, making choking sounds, and Papa would hold it steady, muttering prayers, letting its blood soak into the earth. Afterwards, he would sprinkle kerosene on the goat's body before setting it on the tripod to roast.

Nwanyi Ndala did not prepare me that way. There was no struggle, no thrashing. She apologized when the loofah dragged too hard on my skin, and she poured generous scoops of water on my face when soap suds entered my eyes.

"There," she said after she had rinsed the lather off and wrapped me in a towel. Then she dried my body and oiled me with the udeaki until its burnt kernel scent wafted from every single pore, even my nostrils.

The akwete had been woven in geometric patterns, red and brown crisscrossing with blue and purple, then sewn into a simple flowing dress, like the old ones Mama held so precious. Akwete was a rare fabric, one of the luxury items the more affluent folks could afford. Mama said it used to be common in the past until the cotton farms died out during a drought and dyes became scarce, and weavers had to source for products from distant places, which was why it was mostly the rich that flaunted it. Mama had only two folds of the cloth, a gift from my father on their wedding day. She kept them at the bottom of her metal box under balls of camphor so that weevils would not eat them and moth larvae would not grow on them.

Nwanyi Ndala parted my hair in two sections and bound them with strings. Then she fixed the fancy bone combs, clipped on the brass ornaments, oiled my scalp properly. The tress dangled past my shoulders, and she clipped on more brass trinkets that caught the light.

"You are beautiful," she said.

On another day, her words would have made me smile. Now, I was just a sacrifice prepared for a god—the lamb that must carry my people's sin into the bush, someone they loved so much but who they had to give up so that our water would flow again, and our people would not perish. A thought crossed my mind. What if I ran away? But where would I go? Also, I knew that running would bring my mother nothing but trouble. Our village once had an Aja that abandoned his responsibility. The extended family member whose son was forcefully taken in his stead took war to the deserter's home and razed it, causing harm to the parents. Mama was my priority, and I would do anything to keep her safe. When Nwanyi Ndala was done decorating my hair and layering my neck with ornaments, she said it was time to go. I followed her.

We had just returned to the front yard, where Mama still sat unmoving, waiting, when a shadow crossed the sky. I looked up just as a flapping sound burst from the palm tree by the entrance, tearing through the solemn air. It shook the fronds. A squirrel raced down in swift escape. Dried kernels fell from the top, pelting the ground. Even Mama looked up to see what was afoot. If she had been shaken by all that had happened so far that morning, none of it could have prepared either of us for the sight, for the giant eagle that winged out of the fronds. It was nothing like the eagles I had seen before. Each wing was longer than the length of a grown man. Its colour was twice the darkness of charcoal, with a streak of powdery white running from the middle of its head to its back. Its talons were about half the length of my arm.

"He is here." Nwanyi Ndala stood erect, smiling. The bird circled in the air and began a slow glide over the trees. And she pulled me to my feet. "Go with him!"

Mama was now standing. I went over and hugged her quickly. "I am so sorry," I told her, and moved away before she could say anything. "I will be back, I promise."

Obi rubbed his body against her calves. He nuzzled her hand, and hopped on his two hind legs so he could briefly embrace her.

Then we raced out of the yard.

All my life, everything I had heard about the Forest of Iniquity was that it was a terrible place. It was where people went to and were often never seen again. Worse than the land of the dead, it was where our Ajas were cast into. The story grew into a legend, and everyone in my village avoided it. Mothers threatened to abandon their stubborn children in it. Fathers warned their sons from playing too close to it. Grandparents said it was where kids who misbehaved were banished. Perhaps these tales were their way of scaring us into behaving properly. And I believed all the stories.

But when we entered now, I wondered if we had walked into the wrong forest because this did not look like an evil place. It was a festival of flowers with colours that glimmered like the funfetti ice cream Mama once brought home. That ice cream tormented me for days. After we had finished the tub, I slept and dreamt that I was tumbling in a field of ice-cream teeming with pink and yellow and cream and blue and chocolate. A world so impossibly beautiful that even I who was in the dream knew it could not be real. And when I woke up, I wasn't at all angry that my mind had played tricks on me.

The Forest of Iniquity was lovelier, more colourful. Obi also sensed this because he wagged his tail and panted excitedly as we walked along, looking at me the way he did when seeking my permission to play outside. There was something ethereal about the beauty of this place, something about it that appeared as though someone—not my mind this time—was playing tricks to distract me from my purpose.

I looked up. The eagle perched on a low tree, clawing at a small prey. I wanted us to continue with the journey. We had been travelling for about two hours by my calculation. Sunlight had crawled to the waist of the trees in the east—late morning. Mama had taught me how to measure time by looking at the direction of sunlight. Nwanyi Ndala said the distance to the end of the bush was about three days—a long trip, but we hadn't even gone two hours and the bird was already tired, already hungry, which made me upset because wasn't he supposed to be a magical bird? The all-knowing creature who alone knew the path to Orimili? How ordinary he now looked, almost uselessly normal, like we became after Big Father banished Mother into the forest, stripped us of our innate power, and condemned us to a life of suffering.

I should be hungry too, but my stomach was as nervous as I was. I just wanted to complete the mission and go home, but since the eagle was feeding and since it did not speak human language, there was nothing I could do. So I sat on the verdant green grass bordering the field of flowers and waited.

Obi looked at me, squeezing his brows, turning his head questioningly to one side. "Our guide is eating," I told him. "We have to be patient."

A bee buzzed by and perched on a petal. It was tubby and yellow with a furry head that vibrated in rhythm with the buzz of its entire body. I knelt down to take a closer look, fascinated by this insect that was bigger than every bee I had ever seen. And then I noticed that the stem of the flower was shimmering. I bent lower, brought my face to ground level, and saw that the stems of all the flowers were clear like glass, that the shimmer was actually the sparkle from the petals whose colours refracted through the stems.

"Can you see that?" I said to Obi.

But as I touched a petal, the colours dimmed, its lights diminishing fast, starting from the point I touched, spreading all over the petals. It took only a moment, and the entire flower turned grey, then brown, and then it withered, dropping to the earth in apparent death.

I jumped up. "Did you see that?"

Obi was already butting his nose on other flowers, their lights quenching as he did so. He tossed himself on the flowerbed, and death spread quickly, the flowers wilting, stems shrinking, the brown spreading in swift waves. The force of it surprised me, shook me. Did this mean we were already doomed, that we would never survive the journey, that Big Father's rage had already contaminated us? I didn't have to wonder too much about it because a dark shadow soon skated above us, and I looked and saw that the eagle was done with its prey. I stood up and yelled at Obi to stop playing. The eagle turned the vast expanse of its wings, dragging through the air to slow down its speed. Then it winged towards a direction.

"Come, Obi!" I said.

Obi right beside me, we raced down the path as death spread through the flowers, all over the field, trailing us. The ephemeral confetti of colours soon became a vast field of dead-brown. We had just walked past a grove of palm kernel trees when a loud, piercing cry spilled from somewhere in the depths of the forest, screaming and growling. We froze, Obi and I. Even the eagle hung suspended in the sky, stationary, flapping its wings, craning its neck this way and that. The sound came from everywhere—in front of us, from behind, from our sides, loud and screeching, causing the hair ducts on the back of my neck to prickle. I could not tell if the voice was human or animal, if it was advancing to attack or retreating from us. Obi began to bark, his muscles tightening, rippling, as though he was ready to hurl himself at whatever it was that was coming for us. I did not know what to do—if to run, if to stay. The sounds billowed, anguished cries that shook the bush.

"Tell me what to do," I yelled up at the eagle.

It dipped, lowering towards us, then cawed, its gaze fixed at something ahead of us. It swerved towards the angle we had come from, as though alerting us to something only it could see. Only then did I see the forest opening its mouth, the grass parting in the way my mother's full hair would part when you ran a fine-tooth comb through it. Then the footfalls came, heavy and thundering. I yelled at Obi and just as we began to run towards the direction indicated by the eagle, I saw the face of a frightened boy emerge, his eyes wide and round like he was chased by demons.

"Help me!" He cried.

I braked to a stop, frozen to the spot by fear in the boy's eyes, the crippling melting-the-bone kind of fear you only experience in nightmares. He looked just about my age, thirteen, small and lanky and bony, like he had not had a proper meal in weeks. He was racing towards us, running like his bones would snap and pop out of his skin at any moment. He had only just gotten a few feet from the parted grasses and trees when, all of a sudden, the long fat claws of a creature whose face I did not see, rammed into his back, snatched him with force, and sent him flying backwards into the mouth of the bush. And then the grasses and trees snapped themselves shut with a belch, swallowing even the boy's shattering cry.

We ran. I felt pressed down with fear too heavy to let my lungs lift. It was the middle of a hot morning, and the forest had opened onto a vast land so green and flat that I almost paused to just stare in wonder, but my feet continued to carry me on, through the field. I felt as if I was flying, as if Obi was borne along on a current; my heart beat fast, our feet barely touched the ground, and behind us came the most withering sound of the creature whose cries now sounded like a mix of a growl and a caw. I heard the heavy flap of its wings in the air, felt the stomp of its feet. We had gotten to the end of the vast field when I saw a coconut grove, and we raced for it. Although

I could not look back—could not afford to lose a second by looking back—I felt the creature reaching for Obi and me, its cries louder, rumbling, every pore of my skin prickling with fear. We dashed into the grove just in time and the creature crashed against the trees and melted away.

We stopped running. I looked back and the creature was gone. I did not hear its cries, not even the flap of its wings that were right behind us seconds before. It was as though it had vanished, taken from the world, or we imagined it. Strange.

All around us were palm trees waving their hands in cool, calming winds. The shrubs carpeting this side of the field were soft and dewy. I had stepped out of the grove, Obi following very closely, his fur rubbing against my calf, when I saw the monstrous creature again. It had its back to us. It was a cross between a cat and a bird and had wings that spread to the width of a roof, its body as big as a truck, its claws long and sharp. It shrieked, flapping its wings, flexing its muscles. Obi threw his mouth open and barked and the creature twisted around, but before it could charge at us again, we retreated into the grove. Yet again it melted into the air, as though an invisible curtain had fallen from the sky and shut it out in a different world.

"You are not from here," said a voice from behind us.

It was a girl. Only a little older than me, tall and charcoal-skinned, with long locks that fell to her waist, and strange eyes that shone like the sky after night had paved the way for dawn.

"Who are you?" I asked the girl. "What is this place?"

"You are in trouble," she said and reached out and pulled the tails of my hair, touching my face. I slapped her hand away. "I must take you to Eze Nwanyi." She made to reach for my hand, her tone taking on an authoritative bent.

I bunched my fingers into a fist and held it up. "Get away from us," I said, "or I will knock you out."

Obi growled, baring his teeth, making deep warning sounds that rumbled in his throat. I heard the call of the eagle, a high-pitched cry, whinny like a small bird, and we backed away from the girl. We walked out of the grove. The invisible curtain dropped, and the girl disappeared. The creature was gone, and again it was just us, the verdant green land and the eagle circling in the sky. It was all too much for my brain to process, too much for my body to contain. What was that place we had just been? Was it part of the bush? I had no time to think anything through because the eagle dipped and made for a different path. And we followed, this time running faster, Obi bounding forward, his muscles flexing, as though he too wanted to get away from here before the strange creature found us again.

We entered another part of the endless forest. We had been walking for about three hours, and my stomach had started growling. Obi's gait had become languid. He paused to sniff at strange plants and fruits whose botanical names I did not know. He got excited when he saw a doe-eyed squirrel that stood in the middle of a small clearing, gathering nuts. Obi barked, and the furry animal looked up with a bored expression. It didn't scurry up a tree as squirrels in our village would have done if they spotted us from a mile away. It just stood there, stuffing nuts into its mouth, staring at us, as though no one ever taught it the concept of fear. Obi barked at it. It made a face. Obi circled it. It continued to pick more nuts, ignoring Obi, ignoring me. This perhaps terrified Obi because he backed away from the strange squirrel and returned to my side, yapping in that tiny voice he used whenever he was afraid, his tail tucked between his legs. It had been a while since I had seen him that afraid. The last time was when Mama brought him home.

It had been almost eight years since Mama returned from the farm one morning with a tiny puppy wrapped in her scarf and asked if I would like to keep it, or if she should give it to our neighbour,

Chiagozie, who owned a family of dogs. I was sick with malaria, and all the herbs Mama fed me did not break my fever. My ears drummed with the frantic pulsing of my blood and my heart, and my breath was always hot. Everything hurt, the feel of my clothes against my skin, the scratch of our bedsheet, even the brush of air against my calves. When I carried the puppy in my arms, I noticed that its breathing matched the rhythm of my pulse, and so I named it Obi: *heart*. My heart. And he became my brother. We remained together all through the years, eight adventurous years, which I didn't know how they would have gone, especially when Papa died, if Obi wasn't my brother.

Once, during another bout of illness, this time malaria and typhoid five years ago, I dreamt that I was lying in our bed when our fridge caught fire. The flames licked our curtains, our ceiling. I wanted to jump out and run before the fire got to me, but I was too weak. My bones were soft as though they had turned to rubber. And then Obi bounded into our room, clamped his teeth on the hem of my dress, and dragged me outside just as our ceiling collapsed. When I woke up, my fever broke, and my stomach was no longer revolted by the smell of fried onions or other foods. I gradually got better. We had been through many things together, Obi and I. The weirdest thing about it all was that he was always there when I needed him, which sometimes made me sad because the first time he snagged his leg in a trap set for rodents, I wasn't there to help him. He would have lost the leg if Chiagozie hadn't heard his cry and freed him, then treated him.

Now he walked beside me, sticking very close, looking up when I looked up, tracing the slow circling of the eagle with me. The sun hurt my eyes, and Obi panted, tired. I stopped walking and he stopped too. We looked around. There was no stream in sight, nowhere to fetch something to drink, and I didn't know the fruits on this side, if they were safe to eat and if Obi would be allergic to them. I should have asked Nwanyi Ndala about what we would eat, but everything had happened so fast, as if I'd been a trance. If I had been clear-headed enough, I would have brought Obi's food. I would have prepared even my own food. I looked down. Obi was staring up at me, his head tilted to a side, his eyes quizzical in a way that asked if I was okay. I knelt down and held him, and he melted against me. He burrowed his head into the crook of my neck, his breathing heavy. Tears pricked my eyes. My brother was tired, and I didn't have water or food for him. I felt useless, stupid. I looked around, searching for anything, just anything, to give him, to keep us strong until we got to Orimili.

He barked at something, and I turned in that direction and saw it: a lone mango tree, short and plump like an overfed kid, the type of mango you would find in the compounds of the rich folks in Okwu Village. The type they fed extra doses of fertilizers. Unlike our tall, lanky ones that strained for nourishment from our often-parched soil, taking years to bear fruit. And even when they did, the fruits rotted before they ripened or shrank before they had fully matured.

We raced to the tree and found that lying around it were freshly dropped mangoes. They were fat and fleshy and yellow and red, like the expensive ones Mama once bought from the market the day she made enough profit from her vegetables. I snatched one fat mango and peeled with my fingers while Obi brought out his tongue, panting. He sat ready on his haunches, waiting for me to feed him. I tasted the fruit first, to be sure that it was an actual mango. Its sweetness exploded on my tongue. My eyes watered with satisfaction. It was better than all the mangoes I had ever eaten, the flesh so soft and buttery, melting in my mouth after just a few munches. This was the kind of mangos the people on Okwu Village probably used in their sorbet, a dessert for rich people I once saw in Papa's old magazine.

When I brought one end of the fruit to Obi's mouth, he bit in slowly, gradually, even though he was terribly hungry. Then he relaxed a little more, as though he too could not believe the sweetness. He ate hungrily, but carefully, chewing around the stone, my wise brother. He knew I would have diced it up for him if I had a knife. I tossed the fruit and got another one. My mouth watered, my stomach gurgling, but I wanted him to eat to his fill first. I wanted to put him before myself, like he always did for me.

When we finished eating, we resumed our walk. The eagle was gliding, circling back and forth so that we could catch up with its pace. What a kind bird, I thought.

"Thank you," I yelled at him, hoping he heard, hoping he understood that I was happy he felt our plight and so waited for us to find some food.

We had reached the end of the field, a few paces from a palm kernel grove when I noticed something funny about the soil. It was so soft that the earth gave, and my feet sank deeper. Just as I thought I felt something shift under me, perhaps a wooden contraption or metal, the bottom fell away, and we were falling into a big, black mouth.

I screamed. Obi cried. The eagle cawed, its broad wings flapping and flapping, the sky a striking azure, before darkness sucked us in, before my feet pierced the surface of a river or a pool or a lake. Water rushed into my nose, into my eyes. I threw my mouth open, tried to scream, and water poured in. I struggled, flailed. Obi was right there by my side, thrashing as a force sucked us deeper. I tried to scream again, but my chest constricted as though someone had grabbed me from behind, squeezing all strength from me. I tried to reach for Obi, but dizziness clouded my head and then I closed my eyes and fell into black quiet.

# TWO

# LOST

**I WOKE** up in a strange bed, looked up, and saw Obi flicking his tongue over my face. He cried the way he wept three years ago after I fell off a coconut tree and broke my leg. That pain had sucked my bones for many weeks, and the mere memory of it always made me shiver. This time the ache travelled from my back and exploded in my eyes. My vision blurred over, tears burned my eyes and for a moment, the only thing I could see was the smudgy tongue dropping from Obi's mouth and landing on my face, his sharp white teeth, his sad eyes that urged me to sit up.

"Obi," I whispered, reaching up to touch him.

He barked, hopped around, excited. I sat up, my vision becoming sharper as the pain receded to the back of my head. It was only then that I noticed our environment. The room was small and fluffed and bursting with a mix of cool colours—pale pinks and cream and greens and blues and white. The bed was thick and piled with pink and cream sheets that smelled like they had been soaked in flowers. The curtains were heavy and fell from the tall ceiling in graceful drapes. And the carpet looked like cotton candy, as if it would dissolve in my mouth if I brought my tongue to it. The walls were

decorated with paintings of children about my age. There was something about their eyes, the way they furrowed their brows, and
their sour expressions, even though the paintings were done in bold
strokes of bright colours. I wondered who those children were and
if the room belonged to them. Perhaps their parents had found Obi
and me and brought us here to take care of us. There was nothing
frightening in the space, just subtle colours and fluffy fabrics and a
soft floor and tall curtain that fell to the floor in dignified grace. And
that made me feel less anxious.

Obi barked at the door. It was wide and cream and locked; there
was no doorknob on our side of the room. My panic began to rise.
The people who kept us should hear, should come, and open the
door for us. I jumped off the bed and brought my fists against the
door. I yelled for someone, anyone, to open up and let us out, but
the door did not shake. It only made a dull thud, no matter how hard
I pounded. Obi barked and pawed at it, but it stood solid, unshaken,
and our cries were trapped inside the room. I brought my ear to it,
listened for sounds to get a sense of where we were. But the wood
would not budge. All I heard was the racing of my pulse and the
pounding of blood in my ears. The knot in my throat began to swell.
It finally dawned on me: We were trapped. We were in a sort of jail,
or a prison, cut off from the world, cut off from our people, and our
journey of atonement.

I banged on the door again. Obi howled as loud as his voice
could carry, but the sound only bounced around us, trapped inside
with us, and not a single sound from the outside flitted inside, nothing to give us an inkling of the world outside. My heart had begun
to make funny flips, and the usual anxiety made my hands shiver,
so I bunched them into fists and banged as hard as I could, yelling
for someone to come and get us. But all I got was the dull thud of
the wood in response and Obi's panicked cry. He tipped his head

back and howled at the ceiling, crying in that way he often did when things were clearly hopeless.

Tears stung my eyes. I went to Obi and held him, and he rubbed his head against my neck, brought his hands on either side of my shoulders and held me. We wept together. I had never felt so useless, never regretted anything as much as I did now. If only I had done what Mama had said. If only I'd had the good sense to stay away from the window. If only I had learned to stay away from trouble. This was something Mama drummed into my ears all those years—how to mind my own business. You could never be roped into any unnecessary troubles if you learned to mind your own business. No one would drag your name into matters that did not concern you if you left them to mind their business. It was the easiest way to survive, especially in our world where the privileged exploited our sufferings.

We plopped on the floor and rocked each other. From that spot, I noticed that the only two windows were so high, so close to the ceiling. I touched the walls, felt the texture under my fingers. I loved climbing, but these walls were too sleek, even a lizard wouldn't find a rough patch to clamp its claws onto. I looked around us for a tool, maybe a knife, something I could use to bore holes into the walls. I looked under the bed, under the pillows, under the small stool that held the lantern, and couldn't find anything strong enough for such a task.

I sank to the floor again. Obi came over and as though sensing my growing desolation, he butted my left thigh over and over trying to keep me active, to get me thinking. He did that because he knew that my mind slowed and my body quickly shut down whenever I was overwhelmed with grief, like when Papa died. He took to butting my thighs whenever I slipped into such a mood. That way, I would crawl out from under the sombre clouds and find a solution to my troubles.

I removed the lamp, turned the stool over, and saw that the furniture was built with nails. I slammed it on the floor. Obi howled. I hit it again with all the strength I could summon, and it shattered, the long nails finally poking out.

I had just begun to free them from the wood when the door slid open, and a boy walked in with a tray. And before I could jerk to my feet and race for an escape, the door slid shut so quickly that I could only catch a glimpse of the gleaming floor of the hallway and the green door of another room facing ours, and then the outside world was gone again. I found myself looking into the face of a boy only a head taller than me, maybe as tall as Eche, a little bigger.

"Why are you keeping us here?" I asked.

Ignoring the question, he walked gingerly to the stool, which now lay shattered on the floor. He turned to me with an amused expression.

"So, where do you now expect me to keep this tray, ehn?" He was smiling.

I looked at him and looked at the tray. It was crowded with two bowls of fruit salad, two bowls of rice and beans, two bowls of chicken stew, a bowl of coleslaw, two cups, and a pitcher of water.

"Why are you keeping us here?" I asked him again, ignoring my belly, which had started to grumble.

He glided to the other side of the room, placing one foot gingerly after the other as if he feared he would slip and fall if he walked too fast. I watched him, unsure of what to do with him, if to lunge at him, if it even made any sense to lunge at him since we were all now trapped in the room. Even Obi watched him incredulously. The boy placed the tray on the floor and finally turned to us.

"My name is Chuba. Mother says you must eat and rest. Doctor Achuzie will look at you and your dog after you are well rested."

"His name is Obi," I yelled.

"Obi? That's the name of a person." He frowned in the way that people always did whenever I introduced Obi, their eyes questioning why I chose to call a dog by a human name.

"Who is Mother?" I asked him, moving closer, my hands tightened into fists. "Why are you keeping us here?"

He looked at my fists and looked at Obi. Then he laughed and said, "Is it how you solve your problems, by launching into fights?"

I stopped and relaxed my hands. There was a taunt in his tone, a ring that reminded me that we were the prisoners here and fighting him would not solve our problems. I stepped back.

"Please let us go," I said.

Obi growled at the boy, but he just stood there, unflinching, arms folded.

"Our town is under the sea. The only way out here is up," he said.

My heart lurched against my ribs. "What do you mean?"

"The distance from this level to the surface is more than three kilometres. If you really want to leave, you will have to swim all the way to the surface. No one can survive that. You can't even break out of this palace. So I suggest you sit down and eat your food and do what Mother says, or else you will remain locked in this room until you learn to obey her rules."

He smiled a sad smile, his brows furrowed. He was not lying; I could tell from the thinness of his lips, the way his eyes urged me to sit and eat the food, the tense way he stood. He turned to the paintings of the children hanging from the wall. I followed his gaze and squinted at the paintings and it was then I realized that the *something* odd in the children's eyes was sadness, a heart-wrenching sadness that bled their eyes of any hint of joy. I drew closer to take a better look and saw that the children all bore faint markings on their faces, three short lines, half the length of my small finger, tearing each side of their cheeks. Like the ones on my face. Like the ones on Chuba's face. Like the ones on Mama and Eche and Nwanyi Ndala, the same markings that differentiated us so that people could tell who we were without bothering to ask where we came from.

"Who are they?" I asked the boy.

But I already knew the answer to my own question. I already knew that these were the children from times past who were sent to atone for our Original Sin and never made it back home. And the panic jumped in my belly, a tremble coursing all over my body, blurring my vision.

"Now, you know," he said with a smile.

"Get us out of here!" I bunched my fist.

The door slid open at that moment and before I could lunge at him, he took a quick step outside, and the door swung back in place, once again trapping Obi and me. I pounded the door, yelling Chuba's name. Obi joined in, his howling pushing against the ceiling. And there was something different about his cries this time. He sounded terribly frightened and anxious. I turned to look at him and saw that he was barking at the paintings. Or what used to be the paintings. The faces had all disappeared, and the frames were now smudges of colours in chaotic form.

I looked at the paintings, closed my eyes, and opened them again. The faces had indeed disappeared. I asked Obi what this meant, if he had seen the faces as I did. He yelped in response and moved away from the wall, his cries ending in a whine. He was afraid. Fear clamped its talons around me. I felt a sudden chill, my knees locking, my feet glued to the floor.

"Eat the damned food, Adanne, or don't you want to get away from here?" said a voice that came from everywhere.

Obi hopped and barked louder at a different painting, the one at the end of the wall, and I saw that the face had returned—a girl with a stern look and pinched lips.

"Eat," she said, the words emitting from all around her. Her mouth did not move. Her eyes did not shift, but the voice came from her frame. "Stop staring. Didn't your mother tell you it's rude to stare at people?"

I shivered and backed away from the frame. Obi whimpered and hid behind my legs.

"Eat," the girl said again.

I didn't wait for her to speak again. We went quietly to the tray.

Doctor Achuzie came hours later, after Obi and I had eaten and laid on the bed to rest. The door slid open and shut in a flash and there he was, standing by the head of our bed, grinning down at us—a tall, fair boy with long arms and thick black hair that was too busy for his small head. He seemed to be a year or two older than me.

"You look well-rested," he said.

Obi shot up on all fours and growled at him. The boy did not flinch. He held out his hand slowly, ignoring the threatening snarls, to pat Obi's head.

"He is going to rip your hand into shreds," I warned him.

He laughed. "He'll do no such thing. He's a good boy."

And Obi stopped growling.

"You are a good boy, aren't you?"

Obi began to nuzzle the hand, rubbing his head on the boy's limb. I was a little disappointed, but I was glad that Obi had behaved well. In all the years we'd spent together, he had only once ferociously attacked someone—a man who cornered us in the bush on our way back from the stream.

"I see you're all well-rested," Achuzie said and whipped out a stethoscope from his pocket. "Do you mind?" He held out the device. "I'd like to listen to your heart. I want to be sure you are not hurt on the inside."

"I am not hurt," I said.

"I have to be certain that you are fine." He moved closer.

"Don't you dare touch me," I said, getting off the bed.

He sighed, leaned against the door, and crossed his hands, a mocking smile tugging his lower lip down. "Adanne, are you sure you want to get out of this room any time soon?"

A subtle threat. He knew the weight of his words and did not bother to hide his taunting expression as he came nearer with the device. I let him. He placed the cold metal on the side of my chest and plugged his ears with the other ends. He listened, his eyes roving in their sockets, searching my face. And when he tilted my head up, whipped out a torch from his pocket, and flashed the light in my eyes, I tried to pace my breathing and resist the urge to shove him away with all the strength I had. We were still trapped in this room, and so I must follow the rules. I must ignore that irritating air of superiority he wore with careless ease, that annoying arc of his neck, the way he pushed my chin upward, how his small smile flared his nostrils, as if letting me know that I was at their mercy, powerless, a bird whose wings had been clipped. I took a deep breath. When he pocketed the torch and took a step back, I finally let out the air that I had been holding.

"You look fine. That's great." He turned and headed briskly for the door. "Come with me. Mother would like to see you now."

I stood up. Obi too.

"Who is Mother?" I asked.

No response. The door slid open and stayed open. Achuzie waved me over and headed down the hallway, the click of his shoes hard on the marbled floor. We followed him. The hallway was long and narrow and cramped with locked green doors, like a fancy hotel. The walls were painted a lighter shade of green, and the fluorescent lights that flooded down from the ceiling were an even paler shade of the same colour. There was not a single stain on the wall, not a speck of dirt or litter on the mirror-like marble floor. And the only sounds I could hear were from Achuzie's shoes, mine and Obi's footfalls behind him. I could not tell if the other rooms were occupied, if there were young children like me trapped inside with weird paintings and fancy décor.

We stepped out of the long hallway into a vast room fitted with chairs and tables and cushions and sofas, more plush furniture than I had ever seen. In my peripheral vision, someone in white flitted past. I turned to catch a glimpse of their face, but they disappeared into the door leading off the room. Then we walked out into the yard, where sunrays washed over the lawn and the green and the trees, beside which people roughly my age sat in clusters giggling or listening to someone speak to them as a group.

"Who are they?" I asked Achuzie.

He did not turn to look at me or pause at all. He simply said, "Your siblings. They are having a good time, aren't they?"

I wanted to say that they were not my siblings, but there was hardly any point because the children had all stopped talking and were now looking our way. They waved at Achuzie and greeted him with smiles. But they only stared at us, some leaning closer to whisper into each other's ears, their eyes shining with curiosity, their brows creased in frowns. They all bore the same markings as me and everyone from our village. Even Achuzie. I did not need anyone to tell me that they were the Aja who had been offered to the Forest of Iniquity to atone for our sin. They appeared not to be worried about being trapped here. Their skin gleamed, well-oiled, and their hair and braids were lustrous, as though they were fed by some essential energy. We turned a corner, and I saw a woman standing by the entrance of a big house.

"Who is she?" I asked Achuzie.

"That's Mother." He finally turned to flash me a quick smile.

"Mother? Do you mean the actual great Mother?"

He nodded. "She's so excited to meet you and Obi."

But Mother did not appear to be excited at all. She was tall, taller than Mama, taller than any woman I had ever seen. She had broad shoulders, long arms, and a waist that flared unusually—too perfect—before the roundedness gradually tapered from her hips to the endlessly long, sturdy legs. She was barefoot. In the bright rays, she looked like a statue, unmoving, except for the ends of her cornrows that danced around her shoulders in the light wind.

It was only when we reached where she stood that I saw her face clearly: the wide-arched brows and close-set eyes, and the long thin scar on her left temple that ran from her hairline slightly past the side of her eye—the scar from injury legend said Big Father had inflicted when he attacked her with his machete. My heart jumped to my throat. We were really here, looking at the cause of our suffering, trapped in this strange place, never again to see our people.

"Finally," she said. "My precious daughter and her little brother are home."

And although she was smiling, there was a sheen in her eyes that made me uncomfortable. Perhaps because of the firmness of her jaws, which looked as though she was grinding her teeth, as though she was forcing herself to be nice.

"Come," she said.

I hesitated. "Please let us go," I said.

She laughed, a short cackle that disappeared as quickly as it had surfaced. Then she hissed, stretched out a hand, and flicked her fingers, a soft snap that sent air rushing towards us, lifting me. The wind began to propel me to her, towards the door, gently carrying me into the air like I was a polythene bag—weightless, meaningless, as if I no longer had any control of my own movements, of my own body. I looked down and saw that my legs and arms were moving, gliding like I was actually walking, but in my mind I knew that I wasn't. And Mother still had that glint in her eyes, that look that said she knew more, could do more, and would do whatever she wanted with me, and I would never be able to rebel or resist her.

"Please," I said. I could barely hear myself, my heart doing frantic flips inside me.

I had floated to the mouth of the wide doors when the wind finally left me. It dropped me like I was a sack of something suddenly too heavy to hold up, and I was falling, my knees too weak to catch me, before Mother reached out and grabbed and steadied me.

"Come inside and dine with me," she said.

I stared at her. Everything felt surreal. All our life we had read stories of her, listened to sermons about her, about our Original Sin—about the Mother who sinned against Big Father. She was the reason for our suffering, the reason why a child must be offered to the forest every ten years to atone for the sin and if we failed that atonement, our world would come to an end because Big Father was a merciless, vindictive man. He would not hesitate to send an asteroid to finish off what Mother had started.

All those stories I had heard as a child. All our denunciation of Mother, whose rebellion had condemned us to a life of suffering. And here she was, standing before me, looking all fresh and beautiful and tall; the scar even gave her character, added an edge to her carriage. All these years parents had sacrificed their children because of a woman who did not know how to stay in her place. And here she was, standing before me, ordering me to come dine with her. I snatched my hand from her grip. I wanted nothing to do with her. I would rather eat sand than share a meal with her. I would rather be locked in that fancy prison with Obi. I wanted to say these things to her, but there was something about the way she was looking at me, as if she already knew what I was going to say and had a response which I had not even imagined.

"Go on, say it," she said, arching an eyebrow.

I just stared. I could never win with her. I knew then that she could see beyond the face, could see into the mind, and she would always be ahead of me.

"I will eat with you," I said.

And she smiled. "Wise choice," she said. "We are making progress, aren't we? Come inside."

We walked into a hall the size of a small village with a vast, golden dining table and chairs, heavy gold curtains, cream and brown walls, and fat sofas with gold, cream, and brown trimmings. The floor was a shiny marble, sleek like mirrors, the ceiling a pap-smooth thing carved into concentric shapes, the glass windows stained with colours and drawings—all arranged into something majestic that made me pause. I stood for a minute or more just looking at the hall, gawping in every direction until Mother coughed. A laughing-mockery kind of cough, the kind you made when a timid person was overwhelmed by something so simple. I wanted to kick myself for acting so stupid. But I swallowed, looked her in the eyes and said, "You have a beautiful home."

"Ah," she said and appeared to be taken aback by my reaction, as if she had expected something disrespectful and was shocked by my niceness.

I reached down and touched Obi's head, to be sure that I wasn't dreaming this. I had beaten Mother to her mind game. I had taken her by surprise. I pulled out a chair and sat down, and Obi hopped on the chair beside me, posing like he was an actual human and was ready for whatever Mother had planned for us. I was ready to listen to whatever she had to say, and I was also thinking my last response through, wondering how to play this mind game and make sure she didn't always guess right. What was it that made it so easy for her to see through me? Was it my eyes, how I arranged my face? Was it how I tightened my hands into fists whenever I was terrified? I sat straighter as I had always seen Mama do, held my shoulders high and flattened my palms on my thighs. I smiled at Mother.

She just stood there looking at me, a small smile playing on her lips, but I could see that the smile was wavering, quavering, as if she was fighting to keep it there, to hide whatever was troubling her inside. She held my gaze, her eyes roving as if dancing with me, as if trying to trick and slip behind my walls like it usually did with other people. But I just kept smiling. I imagined I was watching Mama working on the farm, her strong arms lifting her hoe and digging into the soil, the sun hot on her back, how she never buckled. Mother folded her arms, sighed loudly, like she was now a little frustrated.

"I heard your mother today," she said. "She is standing at the edge of the forest singing *Adanne Bia Zaa Nne Gi*. She is waiting for your return."

Something jumped and clung to my throat. Mama sang *Adanne Bia Zaa Nne Gi* to me two years before during my illness when I drifted in and out of sleep. Each time I opened my eyes, she had been there by my side, mopping my brow with a towel, tears streaming down her cheeks as she sang the tune that called me back to the land of the living.

"Please can you take me to her?"

"Only if you do what I want you to do."

"I will do anything."

She only shrugged. "Then we don't have anything to worry about now, do we?"

"But time is passing. I have just two days, or I won't be able to make it back to my mother."

"You will, but only if you do what I want. I will show you the way out of this place, even guide you to Orimili to throw in the marbles. But you must do as I say."

"Tell me," I said, desperate. "Anything. Tell me, and I will do it."

"Good."

She picked up a jug and poured water into glasses for herself and for me. Then she looked at Obi, and it seemed for a second like she was considering kicking him off the table, but she got a bowl and placed that in front of him. She poured him water too. And Obi began to lap at it, making slurping sounds.

Mother snapped her fingers, and two boys and two girls appeared at the door, carrying large platters of foods of various kinds—fried or roasted meat, grilled chicken, jollof rice and sautéed ugu, white yam and tomato sauce chunky with diced fish, and other foods my eyes did not linger on because I was not hungry. I wanted Mother to say what she wanted me to do, and I tried to imagine what it was that she, with all her powers, all that legendary rebellion, couldn't do herself and needed a girl like me to do for her. I realized then that she was not as powerful as we had been raised to believe. She wasn't all-knowing or omnipresent. She was just a young woman banished for her defiance, who had lived in the Forest of Iniquity for as long as when the world was young. She was angry and desperate to get something, perhaps to escape this prison, most certainly to escape this prison, and she sensed something in me that would give her what she wanted. This thought made me feel important, even powerful. I sat straighter, yet again.

"Please tell me what you want me to do," I said. "I am not really hungry."

She said nothing at first. She merely sat back and watched as the servers laid out the platters in front of us, then she scooped everything onto her plate until it was almost spilling over. She dug her fork into the mountain of food, scooped bits of rice and vegetables and meat and fish, and brought them to her waiting mouth, and then she shut her eyes as she munched and swallowed.

"You should eat something, or at least let Obi eat. This is too good to be ignored," she said, waving her hand over the table. The familiar mocking tone was back in her voice, a tone that said that power had tilted yet again in her favour.

I dished some food for Obi, and he waited until I was done, until I had patted his head, ruffled his fur, and nodded, before he began to eat. I did not eat.

"Have you heard of Ani Nke Ozo," she said, in-between nibbles on a piece of chicken.

"The otherworld?" I asked.

"Yes, Ani Nke Ozo. The land of the spirits. The world on the other side of yours. You know about it?"

"My mother told me only the dead can visit it."

Mother clicked her tongue and wiped the sides of her mouth with a gold napkin. "Not true. Only the pure in spirit can see it and walk into it."

I did not know why she was talking about Ani Nke Ozo. I did not know why that should have anything to do with me or why I was here. Whenever I thought about Ani Nke Ozo, I imagined it was a place my father moved on to after he left his body. I was still in my human body; I was still alive and so any talk about that world should not concern me.

But to Mother, it did concern me.

She began a fervent speech about a machete in Ani Nke Ozo, which I must go and bring back to her. Her words rushed out of her mouth like water from a burst pipe: hasty, out of control, fevered. I must cross into that world. I must meet the high priestess of that land. I must bring or steal a machete, Big Father's machete, which rests on the other side. I must return in two days before the setting of the sun. I must do all these tasks, or she would never allow me a passage through the bush. I would never reach the end of the bush, never get to Orimili; I would never see my people again. I would be trapped in this place like the other children who had failed to bring her what she desired. I would roam here, in this place, forever and ever, a purgatory without end.

"Get me that machete and I will set you free," she said.

Her eyes were blood. Her hair billowing. Her dress flapping at her sides. It was as if the wind, all the winds in the world, had come into the hall and were whirling around her, swaying the curtains, shaking the doors and the windows, sweeping everything weightless into the air. Obi was barking. My stomach kept lunging to my throat. Mother was lost in her rage. She had become something else, a creature of old desperation, unforgiving and unbending, what the legend said she grew into before she destroyed Big Father's farmland.

When she finally closed her mouth, when she finally stopped speaking, and her eyes switched back into something calmer and familiar, the winds rushed out of the hall with a loud whoosh, and the floating items, even the curtains and the windows and the doors, stilled and fell back into place as they had been before her rage.

"You will leave right away for Ani Nke Ozo." She gave me a steely smile. "You will get me that machete."

I felt like I was standing on ice and must walk carefully so I wouldn't trip and fall and possibly break some bones. "What if I go there and die?" I said, letting the words slowly out of my mouth so she wouldn't sense any disrespect or rebellion in them.

She laughed. "You are so ignorant, so innocent, and this is beautiful and irritating to watch. Do you know how precious you are, how powerful? Do you know that you carry something so pure, this thing people before and after you would kill for? Do you know that you can bend the world to your will if you want? And you are sitting here, asking me about death when you, yourself, are above death? Or do you want to experience what it feels like to die?"

"That's not what I meant," I began to say, but she turned to Obi and snapped her fingers, and he made a small sound, like a belch. Then his eyes drooped close, his head dropped to his chest, and he tumbled from the chair and crashed to the floor like a sack of cassava.

The quickness of it all was so swift and unexpected that for a moment, I just stared, thinking I had imagined it all.

Then I screamed.

"Now, that is what it means to die," Mother was saying, her voice carrying a peal of small laughter. She was still on her seat, now munching on another piece of meat or fish.

I wanted to lunge at her, to drag her by the neck, and sink my fingers into her silky skin, but Obi was stretched out like a dead thing, his limbs twisted at awkward angles, his tongue sticking out from one side of his mouth. I felt something squeezing my throat, clasping me with thorny fingers, the pain swelling all over my body in rapid courses until my eyes blurred over and I could no longer see, until I could barely breathe, until all I could do was rock Obi back and forth, begging him to wake up.

I did not know that the loud cries piercing the still air of the hall were mine, that the groans shaking the entire floor came from inside me, until Mother walked over. With a spoon she scooped the tears streaming down my face. Then she stood back and snapped her fingers again, and Obi opened his eyes and barked and began to lick my face.

"That was the only way I could get these tears, thank you." She poured the liquid into a pouch of the silver locket that hung around her neck.

"You are evil," I said.

She hissed. "That's what they taught you about me, isn't it? The only story you know about me, isn't it? It used to hurt, but it doesn't anymore." She shifted closer, steel in her eyes. "Now, listen carefully, my child: Evil is an incomplete story. It tells the story from one point of view. I know what the legend has said about me—the stubborn, disobedient Mother who brought suffering to you all. They told you the story of how I married Big Father and disobeyed him. What they didn't tell you is that my father handed me to him so that he would leave our world alone. I was an Aja. I wanted more from that cruel life. He refused to give me what I wanted, despite getting more from me. So I did what a sensible woman should do, and here we are."

I stared at her, shaken by her words.

She dipped her little finger into the pouch, tilted up her head, and held the finger over her right eye. A teardrop plopped onto her cornea. She screwed the locket shut. "Now, I am going to do what a desperate mother must, even to her children's detriment."

For a moment, nothing happened. She just blinked once, then again, then she threw her hands out and thrashed about as though she had suddenly become consumed by strange powers. She staggered back, nearly missing her step. She threw her mouth open and cried out, just as light flashed in her eyes.

"Ha!" she said, laughing, blinking, and laughing again, her breath coming in pants, her entire upper body rising and falling. "You are beautiful, my precious one," she said, her voice unusually high, as though she was trying to contain bouts of energy too much to hold inside her body. "I can see. I can see all the colours again." She walked around the hall, touching the gold, the cream, the brown. She bent and felt the marbled floor with her fingers, her laughter loud like a celebration. "I can see the colours again."

She stumbled outside, touching the walls, touching whatever was in her path. She stopped in front of the vast stairs, and gazed out like she was the blind finally regaining their sight, tears trickling down the sides of her face.

"I can see pink and blue and green and purple, all those colours again!"

She turned to me, her face carrying a sudden childlike joy, nearly genuine, as if she was never one to hurt anything. She sounded like she was holding back from crying. I could not understand what she was saying. I could not understand how anyone who already had vision could not see the colours of the leaves and the flowers, how they could not see something so simple like the intricate pastels of the butterfly wings that fluttered past us.

"Do you know how long I have waited for this day? Do you know what it feels like to live a life filled with nothing but gray?" She wrapped her hand around the locket, as though suddenly afraid that I would snatch it from her neck. "Now I can see everything. Now I will take what's mine. Come, your journey begins now. We are going to Ani Nke Ozo."

"Please let us go. You have what you want!"

She did not wait for me to walk toward her and did not ask if I was prepared for the journey. She did not notice the fear that had begun to throb inside me, squeezing my lungs tight, making breathing difficult. Or that my knees had suddenly forgotten how to support my upper body and that I had to put one leg gingerly after the other so I wouldn't trip and fall on the stairs.

She had gotten to the bottom of the stairs and was heading into the cluster of trees behind the house when the light in the world, even the sun and the sky, dimmed and brightened again. I heard the splash of water, the whoosh of its rush. I looked behind the house and saw, finally, the geyser travelling into the sky, and at its sides were small fountains falling back to earth.

After she had wound her way to the back of the house where the geyser bubbled, Mother turned and said, "You are precious, you must always remember this, okay?"

I opened my mouth to say something, but nothing came. I didn't know what to say to her, the appropriate response that should convey how I truly felt. Why was she suddenly sounding like she was nice, when only moments ago she had killed my brother? But she waited for a response. Her eyes demanded it. And there was that air around her that warned me not to revolt against her.

And so, slowly, I said, "Thank you."

She smiled and nodded approvingly, over and over, as if listening to music in her head only she could hear.

We had gotten mere inches to the geyser when I saw that there was a ledge leading into the centre of its gust. She walked onto the ledge, turned and held out a hand for me. "Come, time will not wait for you," she said.

I began to climb onto the ledge but stopped. There was something unsettling about the set of her shoulders, the crinkle of her brows, how she stood unflinching on the ledge with the gusts of water rushing up behind her, some even splattering all over her body, wetting her hair, soaking her dress. What if she was planning to get rid of me? She had gotten the tears and could see what she had always wanted to see. What if I was no longer of use to her?

"I don't think I want to go to Ani Nke Ozo," I said. "You have my tears and can do whatever you want with it now. Please show me the way to Orimili so I can complete my journey."

She put her hand down and stared at me. For a moment, she just stared, and I didn't know if to hold her gaze or look elsewhere. "Are you sure you don't want to go to Ani Nke Ozo?"

"I have given you what you want," I said, panic thrumming in my temples. I touched Obi's head to keep my body steady, to keep my knees from melting under me. "Please just show me the way to Orimili, I beg you."

"I said, are you sure you don't want to do what I asked you to do?" She looked at Obi.

Perhaps it was the frostiness in her voice, or the steel in her eyes because I tightened my hold on Obi and said, "Yes, I will do what you want me to do. I will go to Ani Nke Ozo."

She did not smile. She just held out her hand again, and I climbed onto the ledge, Obi at my side. She took my hand and pulled me into the geyser. And before I could catch myself, a force, like a thousand muscled hands thrusting from underneath the ground, shoved us upward, and we were shooting into the sky, me and Obi and Mother.

Three

# Rage

**WE** were spat out of the same hole Obi and I had fallen into. My dress was soaked and clung to my body like second skin. Mother's hair was plastered to her shoulders, the thin fabric of the wet dress accentuating her frame. She brushed the mud off her dress and turned around to glance at the trees and the flowers and the grasses.

"Beautiful, isn't it?" she said to me.

Then we heard the spine-chilling cry of the catbird we'd encountered before we dropped into Mother's domain under the sea. The creature burst out from the trees and winged in the air, shooting straight at us. Obi backed away, yelling with all his might. A shiver took over me, freezing me to the spot. I was not thinking. I could not think. There was nowhere to run. All we had behind us were the mango tree and the hole we'd come out of. We would have to race across the field, some hundred or more metres away, but the beast was fast, and there was no way we'd be able to escape. I looked at Mother, my senses taking too long to unglue from the spot and spur me into action, but then I noticed that she had a smile on her face, her head tipped back a little, her gaze fixed on the beast as it closed the distance between us, its vast, furry wings flapping and flapping.

Only then did my senses finally thaw, and I dashed to stand behind her just as the beast landed inches from her, tipped its head back, and bellowed at the sky. It stood more than ten metres tall, the force of its wingspan sweeping dirt into the air.

It bent, and Mother reached out and touched its face, ran her fingers over its jaw. She reached into her pocket, brought out a piece of meat, and held it out for the catbird. It ate off her hand so meekly that for a moment, I thought I had imagined it all—this same beast that snatched a child, that gave us the chase of our lives. Now here it was, eating off Mother's hand, purring.

"Okwy is beautiful, isn't she?" Mother turned to say to me.

Then the beast realized I was there, bared its teeth, and howled.

"Hey, *shhh*," said Mother. "Calm down, Okwy. She is a friend."

"It has a name?" I whispered from behind her.

"She. She is Okwy. Just like your dog is Obi."

I wanted to tell her they were not the same creatures and that I was not her friend, but I didn't. I did not want to offend the beast or offend her. She patted the catbird one more time and muttered an instruction, and it whirled around and flew back into the trees from where it had come.

Mother sighed and turned around to look at me. "She can be scary, I know, but Okwy is a lovely child."

"She is not a child! She almost killed us."

"She wouldn't. She would only capture you and bring you back to me. That's what she does. She captures runaways and brings them home. She doesn't hurt people." And with that, she turned in the direction of the grove. "See the barrier over there? That's the door-way to Ani Nke Ozo," she said, pointing to the coconut grove Obi and I ran into when the catbird gave chase. "Take me there."

"The coconut trees?" I asked her. My head felt like it was filled with cotton wool. Things were happening too fast.

"Coconuts? Don't play with me, child. I asked if you could see the boundary between this world and Ani Nke Ozo."

I looked at her and looked at the grove and wondered if the teardrops had messed with her vision. "But it is just coconut trees over there," I said.

She paused and smiled. "Ah, I see what's happening here. Take me to the grove then."

She shoved me lightly, and I stumbled forward. Obi walked beside me while she stayed a step behind us. We marched to the grove and in the short distance it took to get there, I occasionally looked back to see Mother frowning. She looked terrified and excited and anxious all at once. When we got to the boundary, she grabbed my hand.

"Go on," she said. "I want to see if you can grant me passage."

"I don't think I can."

"We'll see. And if it doesn't work, you will make sure to locate the machete and bring it to me." She pulled me to a stop and glared at me. "You want to complete your journey and return home to your mother, yes?"

"Yes."

"Good."

We walked into the grove. The air on this side was cool and smelled like the earth after rain. And there was also the faint smell of freshly de-husked coconut and the pungency of the palm-wine from gourds strapped to palm trees all around us. Even the soil felt different and carried the faint odour of cow dung.

"Here we are," I said, but when I turned around, I saw that Mother was no longer there with us.

I assumed the wall had shut her out, that holding onto my hand was not enough to pull her into this realm. I was relieved to be away from her, to have a moment to myself to think. I sank to the ground and held Obi. But the relief I felt lasted only for a moment. Mother still ruled the Forest of Iniquity, and the only way I would be able to complete my journey and possibly return home was through her.

Obi's ears perked up and his tail tucked in, at alert.

"What?" I said.

He barked in response, his gaze fixed on the small bush behind me.

The trees shook, the tall grasses parted, and a boy emerged from the fold of leaves clutching an old machete. He looked thirteen, but as he approached us, I noticed that there was a bright fire in his eyes—a defect likely from birth that turned his irises into liquid gold.

"Please don't tell me you are one of those kids who always steal my mother's coconuts because this time, I assure you, she will turn you into a rat," he spat.

Obi lunged at him.

The boy whirled so fast. He moved like his body was made of water. He waved his machete in Obi's direction, his back hunched and tense, his hand gripping the weapon as though he was in actual combat: legs spread out, muscles flexing, eyes darting from me to Obi.

Obi snarled at him.

"Come on," he said to Obi, baring his teeth, waving his weapon this way and that.

Obi circled him, still barking, inching closer, seemingly unafraid of the boy and his machete, as though he had been waiting all his life for a fight like this. I watched them for a minute. What a joy it would be to project my frustrations through Obi. We were lost to the eagle. We were lost to the forest like all the children that never returned. The world as I knew it was over. My mother would never see me again. I wanted to cry. I wanted to lunge at the boy and pummel him until he too felt my frustrations.

"Obi, stop," I said, finally, raising my voice. "Come back here and sit."

He stopped barking and retreated.

"Sit," I repeated.

And he sat.

"He is lucky," the boy said, his breath coming in pants. "I would have dealt with him."

"No, *you* are lucky," I said. "Obi is a strong boy."

"Boy? He is just an animal. A tiny animal."

"He is my brother, and he is not tiny!" I yelled at him.

The boy began to speak again, but he stopped because we both saw the movements in the trees, the rustle of the leaves, the shifting of small branches, before a woman emerged. She was the same shade of brown as the boy with long locks that fell in thick waves down her back. She had the same golden irises, the same shoulders, the same liquid charm. She wore an akwete cloth, her hair adorned with fine brass and bone ornaments.

"You are not from here," she said, passing us a glance. "You come from Ani Mmadu. How did you find this place?"

The woman stared as though she could see into my soul. I considered backing away from the grove and returning to the bush. But these people did not look scary, just offended and curious. And the woman did not seem to be as vengeful as Mother, who imprisoned us and killed Obi with just a snap of her fingers, and who could do more harm if I didn't do her bidding. We were better off on this side, I thought.

"How did you find this place?" the woman repeated, her voice gentler this time.

"We are lost," I said. "Could you show me the way to Orimili?"

"Mama, she is lying," the boy interjected. "They were loitering around your coconuts. She must be one of those kids who always steal your coconuts."

"I do not steal," I yelled at him.

"Ha," his mother said.

She began to circle us. I contemplated telling her about Mother, who most certainly must be waiting for us at the border, but I decided against it. It might not be a good idea; the legend made her unlikable and many people blamed her for our suffering, so it wouldn't be wise to tell these people that the woman whose rebellion had brought the world much misery wanted something they had. But I did not want to lie to them. I remembered what the boy had said about his mother turning people into rats, and panic made my fingers twitch.

"I do not steal," I said, which was the truth. Not mentioning Mother wouldn't be a lie since they didn't specifically ask me anything about her. "You must believe me. We just want to get to Orimili."

"She is lying," the boy said again.

"I am not!" I said, my voice shrill.

The boy was about to reply, but his mother raised her hand, "It is not your time yet to come here," she said to me. "So why are you here?"

"Make her eat the truth fruit," said the boy.

His mother held up a hand again and shot him a searing gaze. "We will find out why you are here," she told me, and the boy smiled a small, thin smile that said he'd won and would enjoy whatever his mother decided to do to Obi and me.

"Bring them along, Uchenna," she told the boy, "I must summon the elders." And with that, she disappeared into the leaves.

"Come with me. And you better hurry up. I have things to do," Uchenna said.

We followed him into the heart of the forest that opened into a small village sitting on a wide flatland. The houses were arranged in organized sections with narrow pathways and fences built from clipped, short trees. The air smelled of cooked food and ripe cashews and oranges and upa. The earth was soft and bore the wavy patterns of the brooms that swept it. Small children came out of their front doors to look at us, scores of golden eyes watching us from the dim homes. Mothers came out from the outkitchens to mutter among themselves, some calling to each other across their fences.

"Nekwa, do you see what my eyes are seeing?"

"How did a human being cross into Ani Nke Ozo?"

"Alu!"

Their voices followed us past winding pathways and down to the village square, where the elders had gathered, a meeting already in progress. Uchenna's mother stood in the middle, addressing them. She stopped when she saw us and waved us over.

"Sit," she said, "Nolu ani." She pointed to a spot in the centre.

I went and sat, and Obi climbed into my lap and rested his head in the crook of my arm. The elders leaned into each other to whisper. I pressed my face against Obi's fur, willing the trembling that had started in my stomach to stop.

"Eze Nwanyi," one of the men spoke up, addressing Uchenna's mother. "What you said is true: This child indeed came from the land of the humans."

Heads nodded in agreement.

"We have never seen such a thing before. And since we do not have a precedent to guide us, how then do we deal with this breach? What does it even mean?"

Eze Nwanyi looked at me, and I saw the concern in her eyes for the first time. "She clearly is one of the Ajas her people banished into the Forest of Iniquity for atonement." And to me, she said, "Isn't that true?"

"It's true," I said.

"She has a gift," said one of the old women. "That's why Ani Nke Ozo allowed her in. She is one of the rare children we were told can walk through worlds without needing to shed their bodies."

"Of course, she has a gift," a man cut in. "But what does that mean for us on this side? She has breached our boundary and may have dragged in something rotten with her."

"You have spoken the truth, Okoye," said a woman who appeared to be about Mama's age, her ogodo hastily knotted under her arm. "My mother once told me the story of the child who walked into this world, lost her way, and never made it back. Every night, they heard the cries of the girl's mother from the other side. It haunted them for years. The girl, so desperate to go home, tried everything, and when those failed, she went raving mad before her body expired."

"Taa, Mgbafo! Shut your mouth!" Eze Nwanyi snapped at the woman. "How could you say such a horrible thing in front of this child? Have you no sense of decency?"

"I am only saying that we must do everything for this girl and quickly too so that what happened in the past will not repeat itself."

"You did not have to scare her with your story," Eze Nwanyi hissed. "You did not have to scare her, do you hear me?"

"Did I scare the girl? And why are we talking about her like she still sucks her mother's breasts? She should be more than twelve in human age. She is not a baby anymore. I had already given birth to two children when I was her grade in Ani Mmadu!"

"You must banish her into the Forest of Iniquity," one man said.

"No, Okafo," Eze Nwanyi said. "Have you forgotten that Mother lives in the forest, that she has been seeking vengeance? Do you know the catastrophe she can wreak on all worlds if she lays her hands on this child?"

My heart skipped a beat. I stared at the floor, hoping that they would not look at me, that they would not see into my eyes and find the truth lurking behind them. I wondered if it was too late to tell them that I had already met Mother and that she was probably at the boundary awaiting my return. But these people didn't seem to have the power Mother carried. They were not her match in any way. They were our people who died and crossed over to this side; they were like us in every way, without human skin—powerless, afraid, confused.

"We can't send her back there. She carries a power that's both rare and dangerous."

"Then we should place her under house arrest and keep her there until we have answers," Mgbafo said.

"You have lost your mind!" Eze Nwanyi shot back.

"No, it's you who have lost your goddamn mind," Mgbafo replied. "What the hell is wrong with you? How dare you put us at risk because of a human Aja?"

The women hulked to their feet, shooting words at each other. The voices rose and clashed. Eze Nwanyi's words seared. Mgbafo's tone was piercing. And the other elders jumped to their feet and pulled the women apart. Obi dug his head deeper into my neck, as though he wanted to block out the noise. I looked at the elders, listened to the passionate exchanges. I wished I had been upfront initially. I should have told Eze Nwanyi about Mother, who wanted something from them, who was at the border right now, waiting for me. I shouldn't have lied, and now these people were fighting because of me.

Eze Nwanyi raised her voice higher, silencing all others. "We will send two messengers to Big Father's shrine. He will tell us how to solve this matter quickly before things spoil before our very eyes."

"I agree," said Okoye. "The messengers should take them along."

"Mba," said Eze Nwanyi, "we will not do it like that. Look at them." She waved her hand at us. "They are hungry. She needs a bath. They need to rest. We will not send a child and her pet into a forest looking like this. Our mothers raised us better than that. I will take her to my house and care for her until the messengers return."

The elders muttered among themselves, nodding in agreement.

"You have spoken well, Eze Nwanyi," said Okoye. "I will send my daughters over with some soaps and coconut oil for her hair."

"I will send over a bowl of yam pottage," another woman said.

"I will send some cutlets of my roasted bush meat," a man, who had barely spoken all this while, said.

"Does she drink palm-wine? I still have a keg from the fresh batch I tapped this morning," said another man.

"Mbanu," said the oldest man. "She is too young for that. Or do you want her to end up like your useless brother Okeke who sleeps in his wine and bathes in it?"

Everyone laughed.

"When I was her age," the palm-wine tapper said. "I was already stealing from my father's keg. I bet you, a girl like this who carries the gift of the gods must have a strong head for wine. Let her drink, even if it is only a sip, so that if she is lucky enough to return to her people, she will tell them the story of the greatest tapper on the other side."

"No, she will not drink the wine," Eze Nwanyi said, her tone stiff with finality, but laughter hung at the end of her words. "Send the keg, still. My body will need some of it to help me sleep well this night. I haven't been sleeping well at all."

They bantered. They laughed. Mgbafo hugged Eze Nwanyi. They looked into each other's faces, pleased with their decision. The gold in their eyes burned brighter, stark against the mud tone of their fine bodies.

Eze Nwanyi turned to Obi and me with a smile. "We will need a bit of your hair, some nails, and your spittle to take to the shrine. That is the only way Big Father will identify you and tell us what to do." She brought out a small knife from her pocket, a tiny glinting thing whose blade was now worn thin from frequent sharpening. "It won't hurt," she said, "I promise."

She clipped some strands of my hair from the root and deposited it onto a small calabash one of the women held out. She clipped my overgrown toenails, and then she asked me to spit into a tiny calabash that was the size of a cut-open orange. "This will do," she said. "Every detail about you and your story can be found in them. Do not worry, my daughter. Big Father will show us the way."

"Thank you," I said, but guilt had squeezed my insides into a knot. For how long would I keep up with the charade? And what would they do when they eventually found out? I did not have an answer for any of these questions and was not sure I would deal with them when the moment of truth came.

"Come with me, my daughter," Eze Nwanyi said. "I will take you home now."

And the sky opened its mouth and poured down on the village, and everyone scampered in different directions towards their dwellings.

## Four

# Rest

**THE RAIN** drenched the village. It washed the red dust off the roofs of the houses and walls and fences. It swiped off the thick coats of red that clung to the palm fronds and the wide hands of the banana and plantain. It melded with the winds, pushed against the trees, and swung in the branches. It soaked the ceiling, spattering drops onto the floor of Eze Nwanyi's living room. Uchenna placed a basin at the spot to collect the stubborn water.

"This is one angry downpour," his mother said, looking out of her window. Outside, the rain poured in slanting sheets, slapping against everything. She pulled the shutters closed and frowned at the ceiling. "We must change it this week. I don't think it will survive this rainy season."

Luckily, we had reached her house on the hill before the sky fully opened its mouth. Obi lay in a corner and peered at his environment from the corner of his eyes. He didn't seem anxious. He looked about to fall asleep, his eyelids often drooping closed, but he popped them open whenever the rain pounded, whenever thunder clapped with ferocity, whenever someone moved around him, or he felt that I had shifted an inch away from him. After Eze Nwanyi

83

brought us to her house, Obi had spent some time walking around her living room, sniffing her sofa, searching for strange things at the corners, as though scoping the area to be sure it was safe, before coming to rest by my side.

The rains soon whittled down into a drizzle, and Eze Nwanyi decreed that I could go ahead and bathe in the out-bathroom—a small lean-to at the back of her house, the floor covered with old periwinkle shells. I washed quickly, barely letting water touch my back, and stepped outside to find Obi waiting by the door. We returned to the house gingerly. We knew, according to our home training, to obey our host's rules. She wanted us to eat with her and Uchenna and rest for the night and had set the table by the time we returned to the living room. Uchenna was already seated, his face tightened into a frown. I would have to sit across from the table and look at his face as I ate my portion of the ukwa his mother had served. I did not want to sit at the table; I did not want to engage in the small talk. I did not want to look at the sulky boy, who, at a different time, wouldn't even dare thumb his nose at me. But it was the talking that worried me. I could never ask her about Big Father's machete because how could anyone even ask that question without raising suspicion? What would a girl like me, her son's peer, want with the weapon, which legend said partitioned our world into realms and was used to banish Mother into the Forest of Iniquity? Why would a girl they rescued from the border ask about the holy instrument on her first night on this side?

"You don't talk much, do you?" Eze Nwanyi said.

"I am just tired," I quickly piped up. To sound convincing, I added, "I miss my mother."

She smiled a sad smile. "I am so sorry. I am sure she feels the same."

She asked about my mother, about how things were on the human side, if the villages were still hoarding resources and bullying one another into offering their Ajas to the Forest of Iniquity, if Nwanyi Ndala was still the chief priestess, if the udala tree at the square still produced the sweetest fruits in all the villages—the only edge we had over the more affluent neighbourhoods.

"We moved to this side twenty years ago." She cast her son a small smile. "There was a fire. Our human bodies didn't survive it." She reached across the table and squeezed her son's hand. "I am glad we are here together."

Uchenna pulled his hand away. "I don't think we should be telling her anything about us."

"Uchenna!" she yelled, her voice thundering.

He looked away. "Sorry, Mama."

She turned to me with an unwavering smile. "Is the udala still sweet?"

I nodded. "The best in all of the villages," I said.

"Good," she said. "What I would give to taste it again."

Uchenna snorted but kept his gaze down.

His mother turned to Obi, who had finished his food and now lay half under the table, his head resting on my left foot. "He really is your brother," she said. "He will make sure you are never alone."

She dipped her spoon into her ukwa and didn't say anything again until she finished the food.

At the first crow of the cockerel, Uchenna knocked on my door and poked his head in. "Mother says you can follow me to the farm to pluck her coconuts."

It was still early in the morning. I had slept fitfully during the night. It had been two days since I left home. I wondered about Mama, if she still stood at the boundary, calling for me. If she slept at all. What she did the night before. What she ate. If she had taken her bath, or if she had moved on, accepted our fate, and returned to her farming and small trade. A knot formed in my throat. I waved the thoughts away. This was not the best time to cry or think these thoughts. I blinked back the tears, held Obi, and kissed him good morning. Uchenna returned, stuck his head in.

"You don't have to come with me if you don't want to," he said in a gruff voice before retreating.

I looked out of the window and saw the grey clouds that still crowded the sky. I got up and Obi joined me, wagging his tail. Back home, this would be when we would set for the stream or a walk around Mama's farm, Obi's favourite time of the morning. Now he stared at the door and looked around us, and I could tell he wanted to continue with the usual routine but wasn't sure how we'd go about it in this world.

"Come," I said to him after I had rolled up the mat and put it away.

Uchenna was already outside, thrusting his tools into a work bag: a rusty machete, a small knife, an old rope, and a jute sack he'd folded into a neat square.

"Do you want me to hold anything for you?" I asked.

"No," he said. He did not look in my direction.

It was a pleasant morning. The neighbourhood was still waking up, and the air carried the scent of sodden soil and the memory of last night's rain. Obi raced ahead, often pausing for us to catch up and for Uchenna to turn at a corner, to show the path.

"You should put him on a leash."

"He doesn't need a leash."

He made a sound, something in-between a hiss and a scoff, and hastened his pace so that he would not have to walk side by side with me. His snobbery stung, but there was a part of me that reasoned with his attitude. I was a traitor, a dangerous and selfish person that was exploiting their kindness. He perhaps sensed this but could not put a finger on what exactly was the issue with me, and I couldn't blame him at all. I wished there was another way to go about this, a way to get what I wanted without hurting or betraying anyone. Many times, I considered giving up and settling for what fate had dealt me, but then Mama's face would appear in my mind—her hopeless cry, how broken she had looked when Nwanyi Ndala chose me, the fact that she had no one else in the world, not even a pet, nothing. How she could never possibly survive losing a husband and her only child in a matter of a few years. I reminded myself to do everything I could to complete the journey and return to my mother.

We had reached an intersection when I blurted. "Is it true that Big Father kept his machete on this side?"

Uchenna jerked around. "Why do you ask?"

I shrugged, willed the trembling in my belly to a still. "We have been told many stories about this side."

He squinted, his eyes scrutinising my face. For a moment, he said nothing, and I didn't know if to walk away from the intensity of his gaze. Obi stood watching us keenly. The air so still. When Uchenna didn't find whatever he was looking for, he let out a tense breath.

"Yes, the machete is on this side. No one can touch it, except my mother. We can only look."

"Oh," I said. I didn't know how to ask where it was and if he would be willing to take me to see it, if it was even proper to ask this of him. "I shouldn't ask too many questions," I told him. "I know you don't like me and that's okay."

He shifted his weight from one foot to the other, his fine face flooding with red. He looked embarrassed and shy at the same time, standing there looking at me. "I haven't been very nice to you. I am sorry," he said, trying to smile, trying to look at me. Unsuccessful, he looked away.

He looked vulnerable, approachable, just a boy of about my age. He was a little taller than me, a little broader, with a stubborn set in his shoulders, which I sometimes saw in Eche on days I tackled him hard on the football field. Our peers would laugh at him for failing to out-dribble me, and he would hunch his shoulders, clench his teeth, and fight me roughly. But no matter how hard he tried, I always beat him. Now, I wondered how he was faring and how he reacted when he learned that I had been sacrificed to the bush. A new kind of pain wedged itself in my throat, flooding my face. I turned away, trying to collect myself.

"You are crying," Uchenna said.

"I am not," I said. I had wanted to say this calmly, but my voice sounded too shrill. "I am sorry," I said quickly.

He nodded, reached out, and took my hand in his. "No more fighting," he said. "And I promise to be nice." He smiled, his eyes urging me to accept the peace offering.

I tried to laugh, tried to look at him and smile with him, but I was betraying his people. I had grown into something I was not, and I couldn't help myself because my mother would always be the priority, and I really wanted to go home. So when Uchenna tightened his grip and began to lead us to the ward to collect the coconuts, the tears poured. I swiped at them, breathed through my mouth, willed the sobs that were gathering in my chest to subside.

We had just turned a corner when Uchenna dropped my hand and let out a cry, like a choke, and raced for a small bush nearby. "The messengers!"

And it was only then that I saw it: the stiff figures half-hidden in the tall grass.

"Someone has taken their eyes," he said, his words cracking, so low that I had to strain hard to hear him the second time. He looked at me, horror turning his skin grey. "Someone gouged out their eyes."

I stumbled forward, dizzy. Speechless. There was a ringing in my ears, and the dull morning light seemed to pulse in rhythm with the horror that besieged my head—it brightened and dimmed, brightened and dimmed. I looked at the bodies. They were truly the two men the elders had sent to Big Father's shrine to make inquiries about me.

"Evil has entered our land." Tears streaked down Uchenna's face, but he did not sob. "I have to get Mama," he said, his voice quivering. Then he raced down the hill. He did not wait for us. He did not want us to join him.

I was still sitting at the spot when Eze Nwanyi and some of the elders arrived with Uchenna. Eze Nwanyi hurried to the bodies. She sank on the ground beside them and began to beat her chest.

"Ewo!" she cried. Her ogodo had shifted and bared the top of her lopping breasts, her hair dishevelled. She cradled the dead woman to her bosom. She touched the face of the man. She threw her head back and yelled at the sky. "Nna ukwu, ino ifaa we mee? You sat back and allowed this taboo to happen? Ehn? Why would you let harm come to us, Big Father?"

The elders pulled her away from the bodies. One of the men snapped his fingers over his head, shook his head at the sky and said, "Tufia! My eyes have seen the worst of all taboos. My eyes have seen it all." His voice broke.

One of the women tugged the ogodo back in place under Eze Nwanyi's arms. They held each other, grieving. The men stood apart, muttering questions to the creator unseen in the sky. Uchenna stood at a corner, swallowing choking sobs.

"We will get to the bottom of this," Eze Nwanyi said, her eyes turning a deeper shade of gold. "We must inform our people and guard our homes. The devil has breached Ani Nke Ozo, and we must protect our children from it."

"I know who did it," I said without thinking, without pausing to consider the consequences of my words. They all turned to look at me. "Mother did it. She sent me here to steal Big Father's machete. She wouldn't let me pass."

Someone gasped. Another muttered. They backed away from me, as though I had grown into something rotten and could infect them with my abomination.

Eze Nwanyi clutched her throat, the fire dimming in her eyes. "What are you saying, my daughter?" she asked, incredulous, as though she wanted me to retract my statement, as though she had grown so much trust in me and would not believe the truth of who I really was.

The tears came; I could not stop them. "I am sorry," I said. The only words I could summon, the only explanation that made sense, because these people who had opened their doors to me now watched me in utter disappointment, the look of those who could not believe that I could turn around and stick a knife into their backs.

"Mba," Eze Nwanyi said. "I can't believe this. This cannot be true. You connived with Mother to destroy us? For what reason?"

"The demon child," one of the elders spat.

"I knew there was something rotten in her," another said.

Eze Nwanyi grabbed my shoulders and shook me viciously, her fingers digging into my skin. "Why?"

"My mother's heart is broken," I said. I tasted the salt of my tears. "I don't want her to die before I get home."

"Seize her," one woman said.

Eze Nwanyi just stood there, motionless, staring at me. Callused hands clamped themselves around my shoulders and shoved me forward. I tripped and fell and they pulled me up, roughly.

"Walk!" said one of the men, his words piercing through the sharp ringing in my ears.

My head hurt. "I am sorry, I am sorry." The words tumbled out of my mouth.

Obi barked and growled. They waved a stick at him. He hurled himself at them, but before he could claw at the first man, another threw a net around him and trapped him.

# Five

# The Seer

**THEY** took us to the shrine and leashed Obi to the tree by the entrance. He howled at the sky, at the elders, at me. He struggled hopelessly against the rope and each time the leash cut into his neck, something died inside me.

The shrine was a small square space, the size of my room back home, walled with igu trees, and in the middle of it was a strange plant with ripe red fruits the size of palm kernels. They shone as though there were tiny lights inside each of them. They droned too, made small mumbling sounds like the playful voices of children trapped underwater. The branches swayed and the leaves swung slowly in the gentle breeze. I looked at the fruits and looked at the elders, who now hulked outside, their piercing gazes shooting darts.

Eze Nwanyi stepped forward. "Pluck a fruit and eat," she said.

I stared at the tree and back at her. The fruits looked like something I would gladly eat on any other day, but the elders' faces were set in cold apprehension, the looks of those who expected something terrible to happen any moment. If I ate the fruit, would my body succumb and expire, would it put me out of my misery? A hopeless feeling clawed at my insides, clawed at my eyes, like a desperate wish to wake up from this stretched-out nightmare.

"Pluck a fruit and eat!" Eze Nwanyi lumbered closer, her brows creased in tight furrows.

I touched the fruits, felt their smooth, sleek skin. They glowed brightly, too bright, under my fingers. They made excited noises too, like the happy squeals of a child after you threw them up and caught them mid-air. I snatched one from its stalk and popped it into my mouth, mashed it with my teeth, and swallowed its oddly tasteless juice. At first I felt nothing. It was as though I had taken a sip of rain-water, before a sickly-sweet taste burst from underneath my tongue and spread its foul taste in quick, dizzying waves. I felt it in my toes, in my eyes. It swarmed my head, blurred my vision.

I jerked to my feet. "What is happening to me?" I asked Eze Nwanyi, but she took steps backwards for each foot I put forward, her eyes watching me closely. The world blurred and brightened with staggering intensity. "What is happening to me?"

I heard Obi howling from afar, as though he was being dragged away, and his cries scrabbled through the distance to enter my ears. My head felt as though stuffed with wool. The earth shifted under my feet. Something warm unfurled the knot in my belly and then a tenderness settled itself in my bones. I felt as my fingers slackened, as my knees turned to liquid. I was floating, a gentle wind carrying me in its embrace, Obi's cries flitting away along with every other sound. I tried to keep my eyes open, struggled to see the faces of the elders who stood watching, struggled to make out where Obi was. Where was he? Did he also feel this satisfying comfort that spread inside me, a warm light that said it was okay to let my worries go, that it was okay to float in its beam, to bring down the bricks I had stacked around myself? To breathe?

I was still thinking about this strange comfort when bright lights appeared behind my eyes, and I melted into them.

I opened my eyes and knew at once that something was not quite right with the earth under my body and even with the sweat that clung to my skin. Obi was relaxed in sleep beside me, his tongue lolling from one side of his mouth. The elders had removed his leash.

I sat up.

The elders were still there, huddled together, muttering among themselves. Uchenna stood some way away, his gaze unreadable, his body glistening with sweat. It was the first time I would really see him since I spoke the truth, and his face was expressionless, his eyes plain gold. Obi stirred. He hopped onto my lap and began to kiss my face and my neck, making sorrowful sounds. The elders heard him and turned their attention to us.

"She's awake," one woman said to Eze Nwanyi, almost in relief.

Eze Nwanyi entered the shrine and sat on the floor. She folded her legs to one side to fit into the small space that was not built to contain two people. The fruits from the plants still gleamed, still droned their excited cries. They grazed the top of her head.

"You are all right?" she asked, touching my face, looking into my eyes. She took my palms and traced the lines with her fingers. "Are you hurt?"

Her voice was so compassionate, so different from the tone that had grilled and scorched me before I ate the fruit. Now, she cared, the gold of her eyes thinning with emotions, her tone weighed down with concern.

"I am fine," I said, searching her face. Perhaps something had happened when I passed out. Maybe this was a new trick. I shifted away from her. "I am fine," I repeated. "Are you going to kill me?"

Eze Nwanyi frowned, looked hurt. "Why would you think such a thing? We would never hurt you."

"You were angry with me."

"And justifiably so."

"You hurt my brother."

"I am sorry. We should have been gentler."

She wasn't making any sense. Even the elders who now watched us from the door looked compassionate, apologetic. I turned to Uchenna and saw something different in his gait, a hunch in his shoulders, the tenderness in his eyes. These people had gone mad, or they had something wicked up their sleeves, and I wasn't sure what that thing was.

"What changed?" I asked.

"You are the seer, the one who carries Onye Okike's eyes." She took my hands and placed them on her cheek. She smiled. "I couldn't believe it. All these years we waited for the one, and here you are with us in the flesh."

I did not feel any different. "I don't know what that means," I said.

"It means you carry the eyes and the power of our creator. You were sent here to guide us in a difficult time."

"I betrayed you."

"You haven't done anything we wouldn't have done for our families. And that is all that matters to us. You never set out to deliberately hurt us."

One of the elders spoke this time, the oldest man. "Now, we need your help. Tell us everything you know about Mother."

"We need to know how to destroy that devil," another elder said.

They gathered around me, eyes waiting to eat up every bit of information I had.

"She killed Obi and raised him from the dead," I said.

Eze Nwanyi gasped. "The wicked witch!"

"What else do you know?" the man said. "Tell us everything you know about the Forest of Iniquity and the kind of power she has." He spoke quickly, nervously. Did she have an army? Did she have an armoury? How many people lived in her world? His eyes took on a sombre gleam, the gold soft against the night-coloured pupils. He blinked often; he was blinking back tears.

"She took my tears," I said. "When she killed Obi, I cried, and she took my tears. She put some in her eyes and said she could finally see colours."

The man's mouth dropped open.

Eze Nwanyi gasped. "So she carries your gift? She can see and walk into worlds like you?"

Eze Nwanyi pulled the man outside, out of my earshot. They all spoke simultaneously, tense words stumbling against each other, chaotic. When they turned to me again, I saw the fear etched on the sides of their mouth, creasing the skin between their brows, dimming their gold.

"We need her help," Eze Nwanyi muttered, looking at me even though her words were directed to the elders.

At that moment, without warning, a scream tore through the solemn air. We turned in the direction of the noise. It seemed to be coming from the valley. I prayed it was just the cries of children at their games, but horror settled in my belly even before the next scream rang out, louder and piercing.

"What's happening?" said one of the elders.

"Mama!" Uchenna pointed at the sky.

And we saw it. Fat balls of fire raining down on the village.

The elders dashed for the back of the hills. I stood frozen, watching as fire poured from the sky, razing the village, as cries broke all around us, as people ran in every direction, dragging themselves away from the danger. I heard a cackle, the familiar laughter that had stuck in my head like a loop—Mother. The voice of this woman who would do anything to get what she wanted, not minding who was hurt in the process. Obi heard her too because he tensed up and began to bark. The earth shook with each drop of the fireballs. The palm trees began to fall. Children ran away from their paths. I tried to make myself walk, to go and help those who needed help, to lead the children to safety, but my knees had locked and turned to rock. Obi began to butt his nose against my thigh, frantically trying to get me to break out of the shock. And in my head, I was screaming at my body, willing my limbs to function. My lungs had squeezed into a knot; I could hardly breathe, and my vision had begun to blur. I felt stuck.

A fireball ricocheted and rammed into a tree nearby. It began to fall, tipping towards us, and Obi clamped his teeth on my arm. Pain shot up my head, into my eyes. It plucked me from stasis, and I finally ran with Obi in the direction of Mother's laughter.

They had camped on the flatland, Mother and her army of teenagers, and their giant slingshots stood pointed at the village on the hill. Mother was levitating, her feet grazing the weeds. Her army worked like organised ants. The first group pulled up the giant balls and hoisted them onto the firm pouches of the slingshots. The second group doused the balls with inflammable liquid and lit the fire while the third released the slingshots, sending them towards the hill. They landed and exploded. I heard the cries of the people scrambling for safety and saw those caught in the flames. They fought, thrashed about, succumbed to the fire, their bodies disintegrating to gold dust that rose into the sky. Mother looked on, her flowing dress flapping around her in the wind, her entire body alight with a fire that burned from within her body. She was the colour of the clouds on a bright sunny day.

Obi barked at Mother, and she looked down and saw us. Although I could not see her face clearly, I could sense her smile, the pleasure that coursed through her as she floated towards us. The wind glided her seamlessly to where we stood, and then set her feet smoothly on the ground. Her smile was wide, her teeth glistening. She cocked her head at an angle, placed both hands on her waist, struck a pose.

"Oh, nne," she giggled, her tone dripping with satisfaction. "Welcome to the party. Can you just go over there and talk to them nicely? Tell them to hand over the machete?"

She stood tall and elegant in her flowing white dress, her eyes carrying only the faintest shade of gold—a colour that was not there the last time I saw her. And at that moment, I wondered if my tears did that, if she had mutated into a more powerful creature because of the part of me she now possessed. And this mutation had changed her body too. It was as if the fat in her cheeks, which had been fuller, had leaked out of her, toughened her jaw, crinkled the sides of her eyes, thinned her lips. She was still beautiful, still carried herself like royalty. And she held her back straight, her shoulders unbending. She would never stop this theatre of horror until she got what she wanted. She had been preparing throughout her banishment for this moment.

"You must stop this," I said. My hands had begun to shake, and she seemed to notice this, because she tipped her head back and laughed.

"Who is going to stop me? You?" Her laughter tinkled, carrying with the wind, echoing all around us. She leaned so close I could smell the coconut oil she'd applied on her hair, even the faint smell of flowers on her dress. "I want that damn machete, and I will not stop until I have gouged out every one of their eyes and razed their village."

The locket hanging from her neck reflected the fire from the launching balls. It gleamed, taunting me. I didn't think. I didn't even have the time to think the thought through because there was no need to and the moment would never come again. I snatched the locket and before she could react, before she would open her mouth and speak, I tossed it on the ground and stomped my foot on it. The fragile metal pouch flattened without effort.

Mother swayed, her face a mask of horror. "What have you done?" Her voice broke.

I backed away from her.

She was trembling, staring at what remained of the locket on the ground, returning her gaze to me. "What have you done?"

I said nothing.

"You!" she shrieked, her eyes lighting up with gold that was much too bright, like watery piss, sucking all the light around us, filling her with a rage that caused her body to levitate. Her dress billowing, the tails of her cornrows hissing like forest snakes. "You!" she cried again, rising, glowing, the air hissing with her strange energy.

Obi barked. The wind howled. Dust swirled, spiralling like a small tornado, circling Obi and me. Mother spread her hands, and a magnetic force zinged from her fingers. She snatched a fireball that had been launched towards the village and swerved it mid-flight. Then she let out a wild cry that sent the ball roaring towards Obi and me.

I started to run but tripped and fell atop Obi. And hell was too quick, too swift, its heat singeing the air even before it reached where we lay. I wrapped my hands around Obi just as the fireball loomed over us, its heat consuming my entire body, sending an excruciating wave of pain that travelled from my face to my toes. I even tasted it on my tongue before it crashed mere inches away. The sheer force of its impact swept us off the ground and sent us flying into space.

A dark hole materialized out of nowhere, and just as we were about to be sucked into it, a bird winged past us, a fish eagle, so big, its wings so wide. But then its flight appeared to be slowing down, even the air, like a film put in the slowest motion, the last thing I could see and feel before Obi and I tumbled through the mirthless dark, a fall without end.

# Six

# ATONEMENT

**WE** plopped atop a bed of banana leaves. Obi hopped up immediately with a cry and lopped off. He circled the bed, as though checking it out to be sure that there was no threat nearby. I got up. Once on the ground, I saw that the bed rose to the height of my knees and was the width of two houses put together and fenced by short igu trees whose branches were blooming with sickly-smelling red flowers. There was a calming tinge in the air, the kind that came after a light rainfall. I knew that something was different about this place. It was in the weight of the air, how the banana leaves did not shiver when we fell onto them. I looked up and saw that the sky was alive with a party of stars and a moon that sat so bright and proud, its light casting wavy shadows over tall trees whose branches did not sway. The leaves did not even rustle; it was as though they were frozen in a gel jar or something harder.

"Something just fell from the sky!" said a voice from somewhere in the trees surrounding us, the voice echoing as if it had spoken into a device that was supposed to carry the warning to everyone in the village.

My heart lurched. Obi kicked into action with warning barks. I did not know yet where we were. I could not make sense of where we were. Towards the north, I noticed a family of birds frozen in mid-flight, as if someone had sculpted them in wood and hung them in the sky. The trees around us stood stiffly. Even the ants on the floor, the stalks of grass were motionless, as if someone had pressed pause on things and left them in perpetual lull.

I slapped the leaves of a low-hanging tree, but they did not shake. They met my fingers, soft yet bouncy like they were cast in gela tin. This place did not make sense. I wondered if I was trapped in a paralytic dream.

The sound came again. "Something just fell from the sky!"

And Obi growled, backed towards me, his ears flaring as we heard the stomp of feet and the chatter of voices approaching. Panic squeezed my bladder tight. I grabbed Obi, pulled him into the cover of trees. He barked, stubbornly wriggling out of my hand, ready to launch himself at the oncoming danger.

"Quiet, please," I whispered.

And he finally stopped and sat on his haunches, positioning himself right in front of me. We listened for the footsteps. Eventually, we saw the figures emerging from a corner.

"Where is the thing? Where did it go? Did you see what it looked like?" said a familiar voice.

My stomach jumped to my throat. I knew the voice. I hadn't heard it in three years. I could tell it anywhere—the baritone quality that cracked his words even in my sleep. I knew the owner of the voice, this man who thought before letting words out of his mouth. I knew that timbre, the calming quality of its rumbling depth. Obi knew too. He whined, cried. Turning to look at me, his eyes saying, "You recognize him too, don't you?"

I came out from the trees, my hands shaking, just as the people, forty or fifty of them, armed with weapons they had built from metals and sticks and other objects, approached us. They saw me and stopped, all of them drawing a collective surprise.

"It is just a girl and her dog," said another voice, a woman this time.

"Wait, is that who I think I am seeing? Is that Obi?" said the familiar voice.

He approached, his face caught in the beams of moonlight, his eyes wide and wise as I had always remembered them.

"Papa," I said, gasping. "It's me, Adanne."

Papa rushed over and pulled me into his arms. Obi jumped all around him, and he held him too. He touched our faces. He looked into our eyes. He kissed our heads. There were tears in his eyes.

"I don't understand," he said. "I don't understand." His voice broke. He sniffed my hair, pressed his face against my neck, muttering the line over and over, his tears soaking into my dress. "I don't understand. Why are you both here?"

"We ran from Mother," I said. "She attacked us, and we showed up here."

And Papa pulled away, frowned. "What are you saying, my daughter? What business do you have with that our vengeful Mother?"

An older man who walked with a slight limp appeared behind Papa and clamped a hand over his shoulder, leaning in to look at me properly. He raised my jaw with the tips of his quaking fingers, stared into my eyes and gasped.

"Odogwu," he said to Papa. "She carries rings of gold in her eyes. Look at her face, there is a faint line of gold running from under her lip to her chin. She is the deliverer we have been waiting for."

"What rings?" I asked, nervous. "What's on my face?" I touched my jaw, anxiously trying to wipe whatever it was that he had seen.

The man held up his left palm, and I saw a reflection of my own face in it. The centre of his palm had transformed into a reflective surface, so clear it was like looking into still waters, the moonlight serving as a fluorescent lamp. I needed to see every little detail on my face: the new rings of gold framing my irises. Not the pools of gold I had seen in the eyes of the people of Ani Nke Ozo. These were thin, like Mama's wedding ring. The gold line on my chin shone like the sun during harmattan. I had transformed into someone else, a strange creature. I stood back, suddenly dizzy.

Papa held me. "Don't panic. I am here with you." The familiar comfort returned to this voice.

"What is this place?" I asked him.

"This is Ani Nchefu," Papa said. "We were supposed to move on to Ani Nke Ozo after our time in Ani Mmadu was done, but Mother had slit a hole in the realm that links the two worlds, and the unlucky ones like us slipped through that tear and fell into this place."

He turned so that he was facing the people—the men and women, the young and the old, all of whom had gathered in an assembly before us watching, their faces now gleaming with a new glow, something close to hope.

"We are many. Some of us have been here from the beginning. We have been waiting for a traveller who legend says has the power to carry us home." He looked at me, smiled. "And it appears the creator blessed my daughter with the gift." He looked at the sky, the moonlight entering his smile.

A boy stepped forward. He looked not more than ten, small and thin, with a head full of hair that was too much for his small head. His name was Nkwo. "I am the oldest here, and there is so much you must learn about Mother and the worlds and this place," he said. "You must help us seal the tear in the channel so that our children will stop falling into the forgotten place."

Nkwo led the way into their village. The houses here looked like replicas of those in Ani Mmadu, and the roads were paved, the walls fortified with concrete, the roofs built from thatched raffia or zinc roofing, and there were no fences here. There was no need for fences. Neighbours looked into each other's windows, and small children sat under large trees looking up at the faces of grandmothers and grandfathers who told them moonlight stories, just as parents did back home. It felt like I had walked into a scene from my past. It was home, but this home was frozen in time, forgotten, lost to memory. A new panic rose inside me, made my fingers tremble, and Papa perhaps sensed it, because he squeezed my hand tight to pull me out of my turmoil.

"If only you could see into my heart," he said, smiling. "How is your mother?"

I tried to smile, but a throbbing had started in my temples—the reminder that it was my disobedience that had brought us all this trouble. "I haven't been a good daughter."

He shook his head no. "You are the best daughter any parent could ask for," he said. "Always remember that even when you feel you have disappointed her or me. Always remember that you are our best gift."

"Yes, Papa."

"Or have you forgotten what she calls you?"

"*My eye. My only eye.*"

"Yes. Your mother doesn't know how to say *I love you.* Maybe because that expression has been watered down, lost its meaning, especially in our world where people take joy in oppressing and exploiting each other. But she shows love deeper than words can explain. She even loves you more than me."

I smiled. "Not true."

"Very true. And I don't have a problem with that."

"The moon is so bright," I said, attempting a conversation, to ease the sombreness.

"It is always like this." He waved his hand around. "Everything you see is frozen in time. I came here on a night like this, and it has remained so ever since. Look at the stars, the moon, the dark blanket of the sky. The birds, the trees, and the leaves. They have always been like this, frozen like they were sculpted or painted or designed by an artist who had so much time on their hands."

"Nothing changes. Nothing actually moves."

"Yes," he whispered.

He held out his wrist for me, and I saw the watch Mama gave him on his fortieth birthday, an antique gold piece he wore every day, even on the day he died. Mama strapped the watch to his wrist before he was buried. Now Papa held it out, and I could see that the hour hands remained at past 2 p.m. and the sweep-seconds hand was quivering, stuck at the space between twelve and one, as though it was struggling to push through the fog that held it in place between those numbers.

"I came here at this time. It has remained so ever since. So you can spend as long as you want here and when you are ready to leave, the worlds will resume from where they stopped when you exited."

"I don't understand. You all came here at different times. How is it possible for the worlds to remain as they were when you slipped into this realm?"

Papa smiled. "You will realize that so many things don't make sense, but the legend says that if we were to leave this forgotten place, we would be returned to the exact moment we were crossing from the human world to the other side. It means that Nkwo, for example, who has been here from the first day, will return to his precise past. Same as me. Same as you. Whatever was happening when you left is paused, and you will return to meet it as it was when you slipped into this place."

I replayed his words, tried to make sense of what it all boiled down to. Obi hopped around, happier than I had seen him since we walked into the bush. And this lifted something inside me. My brother was wagging his tail, jumping around, being a happy boy again.

We reached the village square and Nkwo entered a small grotto where he knelt before a pool. He dipped his hands and scooped water to wash his face.

"The water is not frozen like everything else," I told Papa.

"Some things don't make sense on this side. Go and observe. He is praying to our creator."

"Big Father?"

"The one before Big Father, the force behind the entire universe."

"Onye Okike."

"Yes." He nudged me gently. "Go and watch."

Nkwo's gaze was fixed on his open palm, his back bent as if he would lose his balance any moment and topple headfirst into the water.

"Onye Okike," he prayed. "You have shown us grace! Your ears were never deaf to our prayers. Your eyes were never blind to our plight." His voice quavered. He dipped his hands into the pool again and brought water to his lips. "Onye Okike, we are your children. We are not perfect. We have come short in many ways. Still, you gave us life, then granted us passage into the next life. But our Mother truncated that journey because of her quarrel with our Father. Still, we are thankful. You have sent us a deliverer. It shall be well with us!"

There were echoes of *Ise!* thundering around us. I turned and saw that the villagers had gathered behind me, all of them, including Papa—a teeming crowd whose numbers my eyes could never enumerate and who strangely heard every word Nkwo said, every prayer he made, because they repeated the response in unison, over and over, never missing a beat.

"Onye Okike, bless this child you have sent here to help us."

"Ise!"

"Open her eyes to what she must do."

"Ise!"

"Guide her hands and her thoughts and instil in her the wisdom to carry out your duties to perfection. May our Mother never guess her next move."

And the villagers cried, "*Ise!*"

He scooped more water, poured it on his body, and rubbed his small torso. I wondered how he came to know all this, how he was able to carry himself with such grace. He looked at the sky and shook his head. "May it be well with our people both in Ani Mmadu and Ani Nke Ozo!"

"*Ise!*"

He held out his hand. "Come, nne," he said. "I have so much to tell you."

I looked at Papa. He nodded and assented with his eyes. I walked into the grotto and knelt on the floor beside Nkwo. He took my hands to the water and urged me to scoop some.

"Wash your face," he said.

I did as he instructed. The water smelled like the earth after the first rain, calming, tinged with clay. I scooped again and pressed my face into my cupped hands. Obi hurried over. I got more water, and he drank from my hands.

"Tell me about Mother," I said.

He said nothing at first. He just stared at me, as though searching for something on my face that said I could be trusted with whatever he had to say. Then he sighed. "I am her son, her last son. I slipped into this place after she brought down the asteroid. Do you remember that story, how she brought down the asteroid and destroyed my Father's farmland, how she changed the world?"

I nodded slowly, unable to believe it. I was looking at the boy whose birth was the last straw that broke Mother, whose birthday celebration had pulled the carpet from under everything and restructured the paths our lives would take.

"She waited until the day after your birthday before she did it," I said.

He smiled. "I will give her that. Besides, she never meant to hurt me and my brothers. This is all my Father's fault."

I said nothing. All our lives we had been discouraged from speaking against Big Father, from pointing out the flaws in his decision, his all-consuming wrath and how he tore us into shreds and ripped people apart. We were told to never criticize his anger, to only blame Mother because she made him do it. Mother was the one who erred. Mother was the vengeful, wicked one. Mother was the stubborn creature whose rage devastated our world. Never Big Father, who tricked his wife and failed to keep his word, even though she met her end of the bargain. Now she raged on the other side, seeking the tool with which to exact her vengeance—another layer to be added to the legend and passed from mouth to mouth, down the line, the only story we were allowed to tell about her.

These thoughts flooded my head and stirred new panic inside me. We were not allowed to criticize Big Father, to even think about criticizing him, because the legend had it that such words or thoughts were unforgivable—The Sin Against Big Father, and those who erred would be condemned to the worse fate on the other side.

"Please don't make me sin," I told Nkwo.

He laughed for the first time. "Don't you know you are above those human rules?"

Lightning zipped through the sky at that moment, and thunder clapped in the distance. Everyone gasped, looked up.

"What is happening?" someone said.

Nkwo frowned at the clouds, which belched, unfreezing the birds. The birds squawked and began to flap their wings. Strong winds whooshed over us and whipped up a storm of dust that slapped against the trees, tearing through their stasis. The leaves swayed, and rodents shook themselves awake from eternal pause and chittered in the trees.

"She is the one doing this, isn't she?" I asked Nkwo, my heart thudding hard.

"She is not the enemy, Adanne," he told me.

I wanted to yell at him and remind him that her actions created this purgatory they had been trapped in since forever, but Papa looked worried, deeply rattled.

"My watch is working again," he said, trying to sound calm, but his unsteady eyes gave him away, a rip in his composure.

There was a murmur in the crowd, which soon grew, as tensed voices rose into a simmering chaos, and soon everyone was speaking, all at the same time, the atmosphere choked with fear.

Nkwo looked at the sky. "Take me with you and I will show you how to stop her," he said, his gaze still fixed at the sky.

"How do I do that?"

He pointed at the direction we had come from. "The banana bed. That's where you will find the rip in the realm."

I looked at Papa. He nodded at me.

"Come with us," I said.

Papa shook his head. "Go, nne. Take Obi with you. We will be fine here."

But I feared that they would not be fine, that we would fall out of this realm, and something would seal it off from the worlds, trapping Papa and everyone inside, pausing time yet again—a purgatory without end.

"No," I said. "You must come with us."

"Adanne," he began slowly.

"We don't have much time," Nkwo said, raising his voice to be heard in the howling winds.

"We will take everyone," I said.

"You can't."

"I can. I will pull everyone up."

"We don't have the time," Nkwo yelled, his voice shrill.

"Then hurry up. Gather everyone. We must leave together!"

Papa was looking at me. There was something in his eyes, unreadable, yet tender. He smiled, but it was a sad smile. But then he frowned, confusion entering his eyes as he looked at Obi. "Do you hold on to him each time you walk through worlds?"

"No," I said.

It occurred to me that I had never considered how this had been possible. Now he watched us excitedly, butting his head against my legs, rubbing himself against Papa's, happy.

It took a while, and soon the villagers assembled, and Papa passed down the instruction. We would march to the bed of leaves, and once there, I would climb up first and then reach down and pull everyone up.

We walked to the banana bed. Fierce winds gathered around us. They swept through the trees and pulled and pushed; they uprooted small shrubs and flung them at our linked bodies. The palms drove their fronds in violent slashes, the weak fronds snapping and plummeting towards us as we walked past. They crashed over our heads and scratched our shoulders. A twig snagged itself against my bare arm, and I felt blood trickling down, but I did not cry out or look at the injury because I had a more important job to do: making sure we'd all get out of Ani Nchefu together, leaving no one behind.

Every now and then someone would scream when they stumbled on tree stumps or fell, and their neighbour would yell, "Wait!" And we would wait until the fallen stood up again before continuing our walk into the forest. It was a short trek, no longer than ten minutes, but it felt longer, doubt creeping into my mind, making me question my own decision.

Papa perhaps sensed my apprehension because he said, "We are almost there. We will make it."

The woman beside him repeated the prayer, this time in a song. Soon, everyone lifted their voices. "*We will make it!*" rang all around us, a hopeful song. It carried us out of the storm with Obi circling us, herding us to the bed of leaves.

We got to the bed of banana leaves and the winds finally subsided. A small cloud—the rip in the realm—hovered just above the bed. It rumbled, whirled. I climbed onto the bed, my head poking through the cloud, and I saw that it was a hole in the forest in Ani Nke Ozo. I climbed up and the first thing I saw was the fish eagle, just as we had left it, still circling across the sky, but no longer trapped in slow motion as before.

Nothing had changed in Ani Nke Ozo. Everything had been on pause, awaiting my return, and the ease with which things resumed from when time stopped left me breathless. The forest was still on fire, palm trees hissed to their deaths. The sky darkened the clouds with smoke. The people were still scrambling for safety, their cries piercing in the chaos and destruction. I looked around and saw that Mother and her army were advancing towards the hill, from where came defensive strikes by the people. They hurled stones at Mother, firing arrows at her army, knocking down her slingshots. Mother's growls thundered as she pushed forward.

I reached down and pulled Papa up. He looked around, his eyes widening in shock at the destruction that welcomed him.

"We must hurry," he said. "We have to stop her."

I began to say yes, but I stopped. Papa was transforming right before my eyes. His irises caught the fires in the bush and filled up with gold, his body took on a clay sheen. He peered into my eyes, seeking his reflection.

"I can see my reflection," he whispered, his voice cracking. "I am changing," he said again, tears pooling in his eyes.

I hugged him. I knew what this meant. He had fully moved on, right there in front of me. My heart scudded hard. When I went to wake him the year before and he lay stiff, I had thought he was playing pranks on me again because, you see, Papa was a very funny and playful man. He also enjoyed playing hide and seek—games Mama often teased him were too childish. We built my toy train by grating the bottoms off our old tins. We went on walks in the morning with Obi. I would crawl under his big sweater when harmattan pounded on our windows. My heart always lifted on his return from the farm. The days had been gloomy without his laughter and pranks. Now, seeing him and knowing he would not be able to go home with me, was like a second death. I held onto him.

And for a while, we stood like that, even as the world burned around us. And then he broke the hug and wiped his tears. "The others are waiting."

"Yes," I said. "Hold my hand."

He did, forming a link. Then we dipped our free hands into the hole and pulled Nkwo up. And one by one, the villagers climbed out, their bodies transforming as they did so.

It took a lifetime, maybe half an hour, maybe more, before the last person, a small girl called Nonye who looked not much older than eight, climbed out of the hole. She peeped into the canal and yelled at the world underneath: "Obi, hurry!"

My heart leapt wildly. In my anxiousness to ensure everyone's escape, I had forgotten the one I called my brother. I had put myself and my feelings before him. I snatched my hand from Papa's grip and was about to dive back into the hole when Obi stuck his head out, his teeth clenching onto a wooden doll. I pulled him up, and we fell to the grass.

"Where did you go?" I asked him, blinking away my tears.

He wriggled away, hurried over to Nonye, and dropped the doll at her feet. She picked it up and flung it into the bush. Obi raced happily to retrieve it and returned to continue the game of fetch.

"He is fine. He is a happy boy." Papa pulled me up frantically. "Something is not right over there," he said, pointing.

A commotion had broken out at the bottom of the hill. The noise coursed, drawing the attention of all who climbed out of Ani Nchefu with us. We raced towards the chaos and saw that Mother's army had all dispersed, their giant slingshots abandoned or smashed to pieces. And there amidst the carnage stood Mother, still bleeding gold from her eyes, thrashing about blindly, raging incoherently. Nkwo emerged from the crowd that had gathered around her, out of breath, and shivering.

"She has gone blind," he said, moving close to her. He looked so tiny standing there in front of her as she flailed and stumbled. He approached her carefully and touched her hand. "Mother," he said.

She swung at him and sent him tumbling to the ground. "Who

are you?" she cried, drawing her hands into fists, unsteady on her feet, gold tears streaking down her cheeks, staining her neck. "Show your face, you wimp. Show me what you got!"

He stood up again, rubbing mud off the back of his hands. "It is me, Mother," he said. "Nkwo, your last son. Have you forgotten me so quickly? Do you no longer remember my voice?"

She swayed and stumbled, her brows coming together. "Liar," she said, but she had relaxed her hands. And now, making towards the sound of his voice, she reached out as if to hold him. "Liar," she cried again.

Watchfully, he went to her and held her hand. She stood stiffly, reluctant. "Touch my face." He moved her fingers over the topography of his nose and eyes and lips, her face folding, gold tears pouring down in thick rivulets. "I have been waiting for you, Mother."

She went on her knees. She held him. She cupped his face with both hands and searched him, even though she could no longer see. The gold had stopped leaking and when she turned briefly in my direction, I noticed that her irises and pupils were gone and only the whites remained.

"I see only shadows," she said, mournfully.

"It is all right," Nkwo whispered. "We will find a solution. But you must come with us now." He tried to pull her up, but she resisted him.

"Not until I have that damned machete. Not until I have what I want!"

Gently, he begged her, said they had to leave before Eze Nwanyi's people—the people of Ani Nke Ozo—found her. "There is still time," he said. "We must get you to safety. You have all the time in the world to get the machete."

He turned to Papa and me and the people from Ani Nchefu. "Help us, please."

"Who are those?" she said, turning here and there, struggling to see. Her eyes looked so eerie, as though they had been painted over with white chalk.

"Adanne and her—"

"That foolish child! Where is she? Where is that foolish child? Bring her to me so I can rip her to shreds with these hands!" The tears had resumed, transparent and human this time, but she stubbornly did not sob. She only raved and threatened. At the top of the hill, Eze Nwanyi and her people had emerged from their hiding places and were gathering into a mob.

Papa went to Mother. "Come with us," he pleaded. "We must leave right now."

"I can take us into the Forest of Iniquity," I said. "They won't be able to cross the border."

"We won't go with you," said Odogwu, one of the people who had climbed out with us. "Our journey is complete. We thank you. We wish you the very best."

He turned and started walking away. For a moment, he walked alone, and then another person nodded at me and joined him. Then another and another. And gradually, the crowd thinned out until it was just me and Papa, Nkwo, and two other men who smiled at us.

"We haven't finished our business," said the first man to Papa, who I would later learn was Okeocha.

"Yes, we still have that unfinished business," said the second one, a doctor, Chidiugo. Nonye's father. He held his daughter's hand. She giggled as she tossed her doll and Obi ran to fetch it, pleased.

Papa smiled. He took Mother's hand and led her out of the open area. Okeocha joined, holding her other hand. And together, we hastened to the palm grove.

When we got to the border, I held Papa's hand, and everyone held each other to form a long link.

I stepped out of the grove and they all came out too, everyone maintaining the link until the last person, including Obi, was safely back in the Forest of Iniquity.

"I think my tears did something to Mother's eyes," I told Papa and Nkwo.

Chidiugo tended to her. He had been a doctor in the life before and now did not appreciate being asked to examine the woman he once reviled. Mother did not help matters. She slapped his hand away when he tried to touch her face. She spat when he told her to stay still. She called him a *spineless idiot* when he abandoned the duty and returned to sit with his friend. Papa went over and pleaded with him, and he returned to check her eyes, clearly shutting his ears to her frustrated curses.

"No one would be happy losing their sight just like that," Papa said.

"I think my tears did that to her," I said again. "Maybe I should give her some more and see if it will reverse the blindness."

"No!" Nkwo cried. "You've done enough." His words stung, heavy with accusations.

Papa sensed this too. "What's there to lose?" he said. "She is already blind. Either the tears work, or they don't work."

Nkwo considered this for a moment. In our village, elders like Papa would not even bother to seek children's consent before they did what adults do, but here was Papa, pleading with the child with kind eyes. Perhaps because Nkwo, despite his presumed age, was an ancestor, a figure to be revered.

Nkwo finally agreed. "Okay. How do we get the tears?"

Obi was far off, playing fetch with Nonye. He didn't have to get hurt to draw my tears. I wondered how to make my eyes water. Nothing came.

"I need to cry, but I can't think how to make it happen."

"Think of something that should make you cry," Papa said.

I tried, thought hard, but nothing came to mind. I remembered Mama's face when Nwanyi Ndala chose me and all I felt was rage, nothing close enough to make me cry.

"It's not working."

"I'll help," Nkwo said. Before I could catch my breath, he slapped me with a force I didn't know he carried, a force that sent my head flying back.

"Take it easy!" Papa yelled, hulking over him.

My face burned. The pain shot to the back of my head and tears burned my eyes. Papa collected them in a leaf and went over to Mother, who lay on the grass, white eyes turned to the sky.

"What the hell are you doing to me?" She cursed when Papa knelt down beside her.

Nkwo held her hand. "Healing you, Mother."

"With what?" She struggled, tried to free herself.

The doctor came and held her down. She flicked her fingers, the way she did in the past when she killed and resurrected Obi, when she showed off her glory in the bush and in Ani Nke Ozo, but nothing happened this time. Like her eyes, her powers were gone. She had become human, uselessly human. The realization must have knocked the air out of her because she slumped back on the grass and lay pliant. And I felt a pang of emotion for her.

Papa dropped the tears in the first eye, and then the second. Then he stood back and waited. And waited. A moment passed, then an even longer moment. My face burned, an ache pounding in my left temple.

"It didn't work," Nkwo said, his voice breaking.

Mother turned on her side, curled into a ball——the most defeated I had ever seen her. She too had hoped for the return of her sight, and the disappointment seemed to have shrunk her.

"Why?" Papa whispered, turning to me. "You still have the gold rings. You still have gold on your chin."

"Maybe something inside me doesn't want to help this time." I stared at him, crushed by the worry in his eyes. "We could try again."

"I am not letting anyone hurt you again for this woman."

A memory came: the emotions I had felt when Mother killed Obi, emotions that were not from pain, rather from love and loss. "I'm thinking we didn't do it right."

"Do what?"

And I told him, explained what I had felt. Getting the tears was easier this time. All I had to do was look at Papa and the compassion in his eyes, listen to the tenderness in his voice, how he had not changed a bit since he left our human world, and now here he was, fully transformed into a being that belonged on the other side, with his gold eyes and gleaming skin, those unhuman features that set him apart, so different from me. And the tears came. Papa collected them and took them to Mother. She did not resist this time. He pinched the tail of the leaf into a funnel and dropped tears into each eye. We waited. She lay that way, facing the sky, doing nothing, saying nothing. The air so still one could slice it with a knife.

"Did it work?" I asked Papa.

"I don't know," he whispered.

"Mother," Nkwo said, holding her hand.

And she reached up, as if to catch the sky. Then she dropped her hand again. Gold melded with her tears. I clenched Papa's hand.

"The sky is so beautiful today," she said and sat up. She looked at all of us, sitting or kneeling there in the bush, our mouths shaped in surprise. She snorted. "You are so skinny," she said to Nkwo. "Didn't they give you food wherever they kept you?"

And Nkwo flung himself into her arms.

# Seven

# Forest Children

**THE PLAN** was to sneak into Ani Nke Ozo before the crow of the first cock, get to the shrine, and steal the machete. But getting Mother to even speak to me had become an onerous affair. She didn't care that my tears restored her sight.

"That silly girl almost ruined me," she raged.

Nkwo was trying to make her see reason when suddenly she floated over to me, all alight with her old glory, her feet gliding over the grass, her eyes turning pure white. I sat there on the grass with Papa, panicked.

"You silly, wily child," she snarled.

"So what are you going to be left with when you harm her?" Papa stood up to her. "She is now your eyes. She is the only reason your power has returned. Without her, you are nothing."

"All I need is to keep her crying—"

"It doesn't work that way," I said, my voice so low.

She inched closer, her lights harsh against my eyes. "What did you say?"

I looked at her, tried to stay composed, not to stutter when I spoke. I gripped Papa's hand to steady myself.

"I asked what did you say to me?" Her voice took on a menacing tone.

"Leave her alone," Papa said.

She ignored him. She was so beautiful and resplendent and yet I could see she was anxious.

"Tears that come from a place of pain don't work," I said. "We tried it already."

"Huh?" She cocked her head, visibly shaken.

"I have to care enough to cry, or you will remain blind and human and useless like everyone else." I spoke slowly, but my words came out firm.

This at least got through her rage because her lights dimmed and she returned to human form. "I suppose you have made a valid point," she said, shooting me a withering glare.

"And you will be nice to her," Nkwo said.

"What else do you all want me to do, kiss her feet?" She hissed.

Papa returned to sit beside me. He threw a hand over my shoulders. He pressed his head against mine. "How are you?" he asked.

"Scared."

"Of her?"

"Of Big Father. What if he is watching all this and is waiting for the right time to strike? What if he allowed us to succeed up to this point only for a grand punishment? You know how merciless he can be."

Mother had convinced everyone to agree with her plans. She needed the machete to cut down the locks of the dam Big Father built to control the water that fed our river, the Orimili. She said he rationed its flow when it filled our rivers and streams and retreated. His scarce commodity kept us in line. It was the last shackle he had built around this world, and she wanted to destroy it, just as she did his farmland. She wanted to hit him where it hurt again in revenge for the pain he had caused her. She spoke passionately, and it was clear that she was not doing it because she cared about our predicaments. Her life's mission was to wage war against him for all eternity and after she was done destroying his strongholds in this world, she would move to his current abode—legend said it was heaven, a world without our kind of suffering—to continue from where she left off.

"She doesn't care about us," I told Papa.

"Why should she, though, when we were raised to detest her?" He smiled and pulled me tighter against him. His breathing was ragged, but he held himself strong. "Still, it is a win-win, isn't it? The rich villages will no longer have power over our villages, and our children will no longer be sacrificed as Aja to the Forest of Iniquity. Mother will take her fight to Big Father in his domain, and you will finally know—"

"Peace?"

"Or something similar to that."

"Not while I am her eyes," I said. "She will never let me rest."

The next morning, Mother, Nkwo, Papa, and I entered the palm grove in Ani Nke Ozo. Papa's friends stayed back with Nonye and Obi. We hid behind the palms and listened for movements. It was a foggy morning. Dew had gathered on the leaves and dampened the soil. Our footfalls hit the earth with barely a sound. A brisk walk and we were heading for the hills. Mother led the quest. She knew where the machete was kept and guarded, and she thought it was best to enter the shrine first and subdue the guards before they raised the alarm. We waited behind a low bush, and Nkwo peered over the shrubs trying to see where Mother had entered. We heard a sound, the cry of a child in a nearby hut, and Papa pulled Nkwo down and muttered something about not drawing attention.

The world returned to silence. The branches of the mango tree nearby swayed in the light breeze, and we heard the thump-thump of its fruits dropping. We waited and waited and at a point, Papa himself stood a little higher and peered at the entrance to the shrine.

"What do you think is keeping her?" he whispered.

"I should go and check," Nkwo said.

"You are a child. Stay. I will go instead."

"I am not a child. I am your ancestor," the boy spat. "And you will treat me with respect."

Papa cursed under his breath and proceeded to crawl towards the shrine. A cock flew onto the roof of a nearby house and let out the morning alarm. Nkwo joined Papa, crawling hastily, causing quite a ruckus in the shrubbery. I watched their disappearing backs, wondering what to do. Should I stay and distract anyone who showed up, or simply join them and find our way out of this world before Eze Nwanyi or Uchenna or someone else found us? The elders had planned to destroy Mother and would have succeeded if we hadn't taken her across the border. Her army had dispersed, fled for the bushes. Then there was the fact that Mother was driven by vengeance and was capable of anything. She could do something untoward, something contrary to the plan and that could rip our worlds apart, so long as she got what she wanted. I remembered how she had killed Obi without much of a thought, eyes wild with satisfaction as she collected my tears, her utter lack of empathy. And she was notably stubborn in a way the stories could not explain. She cared about nothing but herself, never minding who was left damaged in her wake. And as far as I could tell, she would gladly give everyone up if it came to choosing between us and her quest for vengeance.

I decided to go after them. But then I sensed movements in the leaves and froze. Something crawled close to me, slithering in the grass. I clamped my mouth shut and braced myself for whatever it was. A snake, a night creature, or something worse. A set of human eyes popped up beside me, and then the figure's hand pressed a finger against its dark lips.

"Shh," it said, teeth a brilliant coconut white lighting up the dim morning. "Don't make a sound. We don't want them to hear us."

The other faces gradually emerged: Mother's army of forest children. I recognized them immediately. Chuba, Achuzie, the faces of the teenagers in the painting, the kids I had seen in Mother's yard, all of them, about thirty or more, gathering, their weapons drawn.

"Wait," I told Achuzie. "You can't go in there. You will make a mess of everything."

"But what if she is already in danger?" He pulled his bow and arrow, turning in the direction of the shrine.

"Wait, please." I thought quickly. "I will go in and get them, and if we are not out in five minutes—"

"One minute."

"Four minutes, please."

"Three minutes. You have only three minutes, and we will storm in there and tear everything to the ground." He looked at his wristwatch. "Your time starts now."

I made my way to the shrine, my breaths coming in anxious gasps. I entered the compound and continued to the grotto beside the banana and plantain plants. I had only taken a few more steps when I saw them. Uchenna, his mother Eze Nwanyi, and a few elders, circling Mother, Papa, and Nkwo. Eze Nwanyi held the machete, its blade zinging with electricity. And Mother was rolling on the ground, grabbing her face, screaming, a fire burning from inside the scar that tracked the side of her head.

"It burns," she wept as she rolled.

"They are killing her," Nkwo cried.

And each time he tried to move close to her, Uchenna pressed the sharp end of a stake to his neck, and Eze Nwanyi held the machete higher, causing the lights on the blade to shine harder, for the fire in Mother's scar to burn deeper.

"Stay down," Uchenna yelled at Nkwo. "You stupid child!

And Nkwo cursed, spat; I wasn't sure what angered him most— the torture his mother was enduring, or the fact that Uchenna had dismissed him as a stupid child.

"Big Father knew you would come," said Eze Nwanyi. "He knew you would one day come for this machete. We have been waiting for you, you vile, stubborn thing." She clenched her teeth, raised the weapon higher.

Mother rolled, tussled, screaming her head off.

Nkwo began to cry. "Please, you are killing her."

"Let her die," said one of the elders. "She is the devil! She is the cause of all our problems!"

Papa was on his knees, his hands bound behind his back. He muttered incoherently, struggling with the rope binding him.

"And you, I ask you again," said one of the elders to Papa. "Why would you, who should be one of us, connive with this devil?"

"She is not the devil." I came out from my hiding place.

Eze Nwanyi saw me and huffed. "Adanne, are you now working with this woman?"

"She is not the enemy," I said, walking towards them.

"Stay away, Adanne," Papa said, sounding desperate. The elders had bounded his hands too tightly, the rope biting into his wrists.

"I am the one true seer, aren't I?" I asked Eze Nwanyi.

She looked at the elders, looked at me, licked her lips nervously.

"She is corrupted," Uchenna blurted, pressing the stake harder into Nkwo's neck.

"Can a seer be corrupted?" I asked his mother, carrying all the calmness I could muster. "And when you say I am, what exactly are you saying? That our creator is corrupt?"

Fear climbed into Eze Nwanyi's eyes, for the legend above all legend had described the creator as a pure force, indestructible, haloed, elevated above all things. Not even his first children, Big Father, and his siblings came close. Eze Nwanyi knew this, feared this force, was raised to revere it, to worship anyone who carried its essence. She lowered the machete and backed away from Mother, who lay spent, like a rag, heaving like she was about to pass out. Nkwo broke away and collapsed beside her. He pulled her into his arms. He rocked her back and forth. He wept.

"What have you done to my mother?" His cries came from the pit of his belly.

Eze Nwanyi and the elders looked apologetic. They stared at the machete, at Mother, at me, their faces twisting with emotions too heavy for the mouth to express.

"I have not spoken ill against our creator," said Eze Nwanyi. And to her son, she barked, "Apologize right now, Uchenna. I taught you better."

I raised my hand, stopping him. "Just give us the machete. We do not want any war with you."

"I don't know," she said, looking at the men, looking at me.

The men backed further away from her, as though to say they were leaving her to her fate and that they should not be held responsible for her actions. They stared at their feet in defeat or shame.

"This has never been about you," I told Eze Nwanyi.

"What should I do?" she asked the men.

But they ignored her. They would not even look at her. Up above, dawn was retreating, the sky finally opening its eyes. Outside, the trees rustled in the winds and close by, I heard them: the forest children, creeping close, their nifty steps almost imperceptible in the sodden morning grass.

"Give me the machete," I said again, trying to make my voice calmer, the approach of the forest children sending new dread up my spine. "Hand it over right now, or do you want the creator to visit you with their force?"

And with that threat, she tossed the weapon at my feet.

"I am sorry, seer," she said. "Forgive my stubbornness, for I was only trying to do what was right."

The machete's fire died. And just as I bent and picked it up, the forest children burst into the yard, brandishing their weapons.

# Eight

# WATER

**THE DAM** rose to the sky, over four hundred metres high, restricting the water. The earth around it bustled with greenery so sharp and rich with chlorophyll, greener than any green I had ever seen. Obi raced down the smooth path, yapping happily, the sun blazing down with a brazen intensity.

"Here it is, his precious commodity," said Mother, pausing for a moment to take in the monstrous sight of the concrete construction that stood like the gates of hell, mildewed with age and time, but magnificent all the same.

I traced the top of the dam, where it climbed into the clouds, the sun meeting my eyes with a harsh glare.

Mother sucked her teeth and said, "Imagine how long it took him to raise this monster to keep out the water and punish his children in perpetuity. All because of what, some stupid farmland? And I am the vengeful, wicked one?"

She looked calmer this morning, sombre even. The encounter with Eze Nwanyi and the torture of the machete had changed something in her. She stayed away from the machete and stayed away from me. She did not meet my eyes when we left the shrine, did not flex her powers as she typically would, or curse in frustration. At night, she curled on her side, hugging her son, whispering things to him that I could not grasp. And then she sang for him, an ancient lullaby I once heard my late grandmother singing. When everyone had slept and the bush was quiet again except for the chirps of night insects, I thought I heard her crying—soft sobs that she muffled in her palms—before I drifted into sleep. Now she kept a cautious eye on the machete and inched clear when I approached Papa. She had become fearful of the machete and was no longer obsessed with it.

"Has it tried to hurt you?" Papa asked me, pointing at the blade.

Some hours before, Papa had tried to hold the machete, but its electricity surged and knocked him off his feet, and he bruised his arm in the fall. No one else would hold it. Papa's friends fled when they saw me carrying it. Eze Nwanyi said she was the only one in Ani Nke Ozo who could hold the machete for a while without being electrocuted and this was because she was a priestess. She testified that her body trembled with its force, and she felt something dry up inside her for every second she stubbornly refused to relinquish her hold on it. Not so for me. When I lifted the blade, I turned it around, surprised at its lightness and the patina of its wooden handle. It was an old and rusted thing, its metal corroded to a reddish black by age and the weather.

"It isn't even heavy," I had told Papa.

He backed away from me. "Be careful with that thing."

We sheathed the machete, hoping that it would keep its power sealed, but I noticed the hair rising on the back of Papa's arm every time I drew too close to him. All through the walk to the dam, he gave me a wide berth, and I had to hold the blade with my left hand so that he could walk safely on my right.

We stopped at the entrance, and Mother looked at the machete and shook her head. "All those lifetimes gone, just like that, because of this blade," she said, looking at me. "Be careful with it." Her first show of concern. And I wondered what that meant, if she had learned to care more about other people, to be a little less selfish. "Hurry up with the business," she said, returning to her purpose. "We don't have all day."

I shook my head and tried not to laugh. She would never change. She would never stop seeking vengeance. Not that it mattered at this point.

She led the way into the dam, up to the powerhouse, where the control levers were locked behind a most unusual metal lock.

"Nothing can cut through this thing," Mother said. "I tried everything."

"Except the machete," I said.

She nodded and stepped back, putting more than five feet between us. "Now please, go ahead and cut the cursed thing."

"Nne, be careful," Papa whispered.

Obi stepped back too, suddenly afraid of the blade and what it was capable of, even though it didn't harm him when he bumped into it last night.

I raised the machete high. It caught the sun and sparkled with electricity, the corroded blade transforming into gleaming steel. And as I swung it against the metal, lights burst forth, shattering the lock. The debris clanged as they fell, singed a deep black. I lowered the machete, and the blade returned to its former rusted state.

Mother sighed. "There, it is done," she said.

I sensed she wanted to say *thank you* but could not bring herself to give me one more edge over her. She didn't wait to see me pull the levers, and I didn't ask her to stay.

"My army waits in the bush," she said and patted her new locket that I had filled with enough tears to last for some time.

I nodded. I had given her something better: a reassuring object to obsess over and on the condition that she would not trespass into

Ani Nke Ozo to wreak any more havoc. Her army had all opted to stick with her.

"I don't have anyone else waiting for me," Chuba had told me. "My father is dead, and my mother has moved on and according to you, it's been ten years since I walked into the Forest of Iniquity. My friends are now men and I have not changed. I don't fit in that world anymore."

The other children agreed with him. They liked their lives in the forest better. They would not have to endure our world where suffering reigned and simple amenities were hoarded, villages bullying each other with resources that ran freely in Mother's town. In the forest, they had their own beds, their new lives, their own everything. Besides, their parents had all accepted that they were lost, and their siblings had all become adults. Everyone had moved on with their lives. It would be cruel to peel the scars and make them relive the pain of losing their children all over again.

Mother whirled around as she made her exit. "Don't be a stranger. I know where to find you when I need you."

There was a tinkle at the end of her words. Nkwo followed her, the edge of a smile lifting his mouth before he turned away and bade us goodbye. And with a flick of her fingers, Mother floated into air, taking him with her. They flew out of the dam, vaulting into the sky.

"Are you ready?" Papa asked me.

A few hours earlier, I had asked him the same question, after we had successfully persuaded the forest children to stand down. We led them across the border to wait for Mother's return. Papa's friends and Nonye had also decided to stay with Eze Nwanyi and the people in Ani Nke Ozo.

"See you soon?" They had asked Papa, and he merely nodded in response.

Now, he asked me again, "Are you ready?" He turned to the levers.

"Yes." I reached for the first lever and pulled it down.

At first, nothing happened. Then, a groan, a titter, that rumble of things clashing together, the gurgle of great volumes of water forging through disused canals.

Then a burst. The earth trembled. We moved to the edge, looked down, and saw the first surge of muddied water from the spillway before clean water gushed out.

"There it goes," I said, putting the machete away.

"Yes," Papa said, looking down.

Obi hopped on his front limbs, tipped his head to see what we were gazing at, and Papa rubbed his head. "Good boy," he said, and Obi nuzzled his hand.

I noticed the slowness in Papa's movement, the slur in his speech. The gold eyes were duller that morning. His shirt was soaking wet with sweat, and new bags had appeared under his eyes.

"Are you all right?" I asked him.

He grinned, forcing fire back into his gold. He was slouched, but he tried to stand taller, to appear strong, when he caught me watching. "I am fine, my only eyes. What are you going to do with that thing?" He pointed at the machete leaning against the wall.

I thought for a moment. "Maybe toss it into Ani Nchefu and seal up that world?"

"Brilliant idea," he said. "I am so proud of you. Your mother will be so happy to have you back."

"Yes," I whispered and hugged him. "We have to take you to your new home. You need a good rest."

"Let's wait for a moment," he said and kissed the top of my head.

Obi barked happily and resumed racing up and down the walkway.

"Yes," I said. "Let's wait a moment longer."

# Acknowledgments

I am eternally grateful to:

Chidinma, Chisom, and Chukwubuikem, for their love and support, and for encouraging me to fly, no matter the distance this often wedges between us.

Nwanosike, the kindest, the most patient, and understanding; the feather on my wings.

Fred and Rhoda, and Ijeoma, Chimezie, Tochukwu, Nonso, for sticking with me, and praying for me. Your vigils weren't in vain.

Othuke Ominiabohs, who first heard this story and refused to let me rest until I sat down and wrote it. This book would never have been without you.

Esther Ifesinachi Okonkwo, Timothy Ogene. You have no idea how much your words keep me going.

Chika Unigwe (Sister Chi!), my guide, my adviser, my mentor, without whom I'll be flailing in the dark.

Molara Wood, for your patience, the tender loving care you bring to my stories. Thank you for making me appear smarter.

The Griots Lounge team, the most beautiful family anyone could ask for.

Ọgana adịlị ụnu na mma!

# About the Author

**UKAMAKA OLISAKWE** was born in Kano, Nigeria, and now lives in Vermillion, SD. A UNESCO-World Book Capital "Africa 39" honoree and a University of Iowa's International Writing Program Fellow, she is a winner of the VCFA Emerging Writer Scholarship and the SprinNg Women Authors Prize, a finalist for the Miles Morland Scholarship and the Brittle Paper *Award for Creative Nonfiction,* and runner-up for the Gerald Kraak Prize, among other honors. She is the founder of *Isele Magazine* and *The Body Conversation.*